AWAKENING

It's Your Time To Remember Who You Really Are!

JULIE CAPRI

AWAKENING
It's Your Time To Remember Who You Really Are!

First published in Australia by Julie Capri 2021
www.juliecapri.com

 A catalogue record for this
book is available from the
National Library of Australia

ISBN: 978-0-6450963-0-9 (pbk)
ISBN: 978-0-6450963-1-6 (ebk)

Book cover design by © Julie Capri 2021

Typesetting and design by Publicious Book Publishing
Published in collaboration with Publicious Book Publishing
www.publicious.com.au

To my three beautiful children, Tanisha, Brianna and Jayden. I love you.

Preface

I always knew I was different. As a little girl, sensing when an accident was to happen and knowing what people were thinking was normal. Over the years, the reason for feeling like I simply didn't belong on Earth became clear. I began seeing intergalactic vehicles and beings, of all shapes and sizes. I gained wisdom from them and started channelling drawings of these spaceships and beings. My thirst for spiritual knowledge fuelled by my experiences of UFOs and psychic phenomena propelled me to seek understanding of my experiences and what this human life is all about.

In reflection, I see that those years were my time of Awakening as to who I was, who humanity is and what I am here for. Many people have urged me to write about my unusual experiences with the ETs (extra-terrestrial beings) and EDs (extra-dimensional beings). Hence, this book. My message, though, is not just about having ET encounters or to fuel some idle curiosity about aliens. Rather, it is about humanity's need for awakening and for re-setting our understanding of who we truly are, what we are capable of, and what life on Earth is all about, especially in this time of global change. This book serves as a reminder and guide. And this time is the right time.

In Part 1 *My Awakening*, I share my life including my spiritual and psychic journey. As with all humans, my life has been one of immense joy and intense pain. All experiences were the necessary foundation to pass on the message of the Awakening Teachings. Some experiences have taken me beyond this 3D (3-dimensional)

Earth plane. My encounters with ETs and EDs changed my life on so many levels. I hope my story will touch your heart and encourage you in your spiritual awakening.

In Part 2, I introduce you to *The Awakening Teachings*, where you will discover fundamental truths about life. The teachings are drawn from what I 'downloaded' from the ETs and EDs over decades and what I have gained through my own studies, channellings and life experience. I have studied hundreds of great books such as *Conversations with God* by Neale Donald Walsch and *A Course in Miracles* by Helen Schucman. I have followed people such as Darryl Anka, Gosia Cosmic Agency (YouTube) and many others, applying much of this knowledge in my path of spiritual awakening.

The information will help you navigate your way through this time of transition. We are in the process of moving from a dense 3D life into the 4 and 5th dimensional reality and beyond. You will learn how to transcend what you experience as pain and suffering and step into new forms of reality with new perspectives of the multidimensional Universe in which we live. You will realise that your reality is not coming towards you but is experienced *through* you as something you have chosen to experience. This is about not living in blame but creating your life with the intrinsic power we each have as Creators.

Humans are moving into higher shifts of reality and consciousness. We have come to greater understanding that we are all equals, living under the laws of Creation. My purpose here on Earth is to pass on the Awakening message and be a living example for others to learn from. May my awakening journey and *The Awakening Teachings* propel you along your own awakening, and ultimately humanity's.

Contents

The Weeping Willow Tree

The tree is strong and tall
and can bend in the battering of a storm
For it knows that the sun will return
and shine once more.
And through the rays of light
broken things will always be restored.
Just like the tree can break and mend
We too can heal as one for we have that strength.
So cry no more tears and stop living in fear,
Be like the willow tree that bends and forgives
And let the love return to your heart.
Have faith in yourself for only
you know what's true.
Let your actions speak just as
loudly as your words.

JULIE CAPRI

PART 1

MY AWAKENING

Prologue

As I stood in the middle of my childhood home, observing all the familiar chaos around me, time stood still. At least, that's what it felt like. Information about the people around me – my extended family – was flashing in my head as clear as day. I knew what they were thinking and feeling. I felt it all to the core of my being. Moreover, I felt I didn't belong.

I shouldn't be here. I am in the wrong place, and these people have no idea what they are doing.

I was five years old, and this was the first time I realised that I was different. These people were supposedly my family, but it certainly didn't feel like that. Feelings of isolation engulfed me. I felt I could die from the loneliness, a feeling I was to carry for many years. Life simply didn't make sense. It was as if I had been dropped off on the wrong planet. Little did I know how true that was...

1

Little Italian Girl

I may have grown up in the south of Brisbane, the capital of Queensland, Australia, but it might as well have been Italy. Mine was the typical migrant Italian family, with my parents and grandparents constructing their version of Sicily right in our backyard. A fig tree, olive tree, banana tree and persimmon tree stood proudly alongside rows of vegetables, which were planted and changed throughout the seasons, subtly reminding me that things do grow and change. Italian sights and sounds surrounded me constantly in our busy household.

I was born on 8th June 1969, the last of three children. As I grew, with my olive complexion, long brown hair and brown eyes, I definitely looked like a little Italian girl. I was small in stature as a little girl, eventually outgrowing my two short grandmothers (nonnas). I am grateful for my Sicilian upbringing for I got to experience traditional Italian family values, some of which I still hold today.

My mother's parents lived with us because my mother was very sick. My maternal grandmother, Maria, would often fill the role of my mum Domenica (or Emila, as some preferred to call her by her second name). Nonna Maria was one of the hardest working ladies I knew. She always kept her hair short, maintaining its natural wave. She loved her percolated coffee with a dash of her favourite tawny port, and she was forever cooking the most amazing Italian dishes for the family. Nonna Maria was the female version of the Don in the movie *The Godfather*. She was respected by every relative that I knew. It was a mistake to let her short height fool you; she told you how it was going to be. But most importantly my Nonna Maria was a beautiful grandmother.

Nonna would tell the story of how she would bottle wine with her father when she was a little girl. And now Nonna and Nonno (my grandfather Giovanni) were showing me, and that was special. The wooden wine barrels were stored under the covered back area of our house. There would be some preparations like sterilizing the bottles and making sure we had just the right number of cork holders for the number of bottles. There was no fancy apparatus to bottle the wine, just a piece of garden hose. Nonno would place the garden hose in the barrel and suck on the other end to start the process, and in the bottle it went. Being quite young, my role was simple. Handing over the corked bottle to my Nonno Giovanni was my grand participation in the whole event. But I did relish it!

Another 'grand task' I had was to pluck the feathers from the chickens that Nonno had just killed during the day for dinner that night. He would sit on an old crate outside in the sun and bring the live chickens out of the square metal cage. Then he would break the chicken's neck with his bare hands. I then had to help Nonna pluck the chicken. It wasn't a good feeling as I had just seen this chicken alive a few minutes ago. Still, this was living old school, and I didn't really think to mourn the death of these feathery creatures. This was simply what was done. Being an animal lover I now carry mixed emotions about what I did. At the time I was too young to grasp that the chicken I was eating at night was the chicken my family had just killed and I had helped pluck.

I was fortunate to have my other set of grandparents living a short, ten-minute walk away in the next suburb. They too had migrated from Sicily. My paternal grandmother's name was Angela, and my grandfather was Salvatore. I loved them dearly and would visit and have sleepovers as much as possible.

Nonna Angela's kitchen was the hub of her home, and like my other nonna, she did a lot of cooking. She taught me the art of making Italian sausages. Nonna would run through the ingredients with me and show me what to do, passing on the accumulated knowledge of her cooking skills. The machine would be harnessed onto the edge of the kitchen table and the long pig intestines would be pressed up against the nozzle to make the sausage. I suppose my love for food stems from my heritage I cherish my memories of times spent in the kitchen with my nonnas.

Birthdays and Christmases were always something to look forward to as Mum would bake lamingtons and her famous apple-cinnamon pie. Standing on my tippy toes I would peer into the white Mixmaster bowl, watching the ingredients come together as she gave me step-by-step directions. My mum had epilepsy and her shakes would sometimes slow her down, and I would feel frustrated as it would take her so long to accomplish anything. Nevertheless she paid attention to detail, being very precise and methodical in her actions. The aroma of cinnamon from the pie cooking in the oven would permeate the whole house. My taste buds would dance in my mouth right up till the first bite. This was about banquets and feasts of our favourite Italian foods at Christmas time; foodie heaven for everyone. I will cherish my mother's and grandparent's recipes forever.

Change and contradiction

While in some ways living in this extended family of Italian sounds, smells and delights might seem idyllic, it was far from it. I would even say it was extremely dysfunctional. My childhood was the epitome of change and contradiction.

When my childhood environment was good, I absorbed it and it was wonderful. Then when things were bad, I took it all in, and it was horrible. I didn't know which way the pendulum was going to

3

swing from one day, or one hour, to the next. And that pendulum swung wide, mostly due to my father and mother.

My father's name was Carmelo, but in English everyone called him Charlie. My dad was a hardworking man with a fiery Italian temper. He was like Dr Jekyll and Mr Hyde, displaying uncontrollable anger that would send everyone into silent damage control. I formed my own way of coping with his behaviour. I would find a room to cower in, or I would run outside, seeking safety. But this was limited as I would not dare go outside our yard. Then there were many times I ended up being in the toilet, not to escape but because I would lose all control of my bodily functions.

This was the not-so-nice side of being a clairsentient child.[1] I would absorb all the energies around me – good and bad. My own fear was bad enough, let alone taking on someone else's feelings of rage and anger. This just compounded the experience, and my body could not deal with it. It would take many years to learn how to not take on other people's emotional stuff. But as a child, I was bouncing off the walls.

My father possessed no patience whatsoever. Even the simplest things like a door slamming shut would trigger him. Our house must have been built in a wind tunnel. Looking back I wish we'd had door stoppers, for even if you were not the cause you were sure to be blamed. I learnt at a young age to run away, and run I did.

Unfortunately, the kind of behaviour that I lived with every day did not set me up very well for adulthood as I somehow learnt to accept being yelled at as normal. I had to learn later in life how to have a voice and to stand up for myself and not tolerate this from anyone.

Despite this way of life in our home, I would also experience my father's love. His Saturday ritual was to drive to the outer suburbs of Brisbane and collect fresh eggs from a farm. He would always ask me if I wanted to come for a drive and I would happily reply yes. Sometimes we would talk and other times we couldn't. But to me it

---

1. clairsentient: able to receive psychic information through sensing or feeling subtle energy.

did not matter. This was my quality time with my father, my peace between the storms.

My dad was a professional fisherman, owning a 60-foot fishing boat named *Romeo*. We were lucky to have fresh seafood every week. As soon as I'd hear the truck drive up our driveway, I would run out the back door to greet him and ask if he had any scallops for me. This had to be one of my favourite moments, especially when the answer was 'Si' (Yes). Sicilian was spoken most of the time, especially when my grandparents were around. I was fluent in both English and Sicilian.

As a child you just don't see things as an adult does. You see through the eyes of innocence. I wanted to see the world for its good, not its bad. So I didn't mull over the bad, even though it was happening at times. I understood what was right and wrong, and no matter how bad things were, I tried so hard to see beyond my dad's rants and raves.

I tried to do the same with my mum. We all took care of Mum, or Ma as I would call her. Besides epilepsy she also had bipolar disorder, and many years later was diagnosed with schizophrenia. Unfortunately, the medications back in the 1970s were not like today's, so my mother was consuming an incredible number of prescribed drugs that made her unsteady on her feet. My dad would always be the one to take Ma to the doctors, and my grandmother would help cook most of the meals. Ma was a Catholic and would often want to go to church. Since nobody else had a real desire to take her, I would have the task. It was always a slow 20-minute walk to the local church.

Other trips were to the city. It was only a short 5-minute walk from home to the bus stop and a further 20 minutes on the bus. I would take her hand and find a seat for us to sit down. I would always notice people staring at us and could not understand why. Looking back, I feel it was them being in awe of us as it is normally the parent looking after the child, not the other way around.

Before Mum and I would leave home, I would silently pray that we would get to our destination safely and back again without her falling and having a fit. It was a huge responsibility for a six-year-old. I witnessed her having hundreds of fits, resulting in many bruises, cuts, burns, fractures, hospital visits and stays in psychiatric hospitals over many years. Living with my mother was like being on emergency call 24 hours a day. Every noise stopped me in my tracks. *Where is she? Has she fallen?* There was always a sigh of relief when we found that she was okay. But this was few and far between. Never did she complain though. Her resilience was remarkable.

My mother's inability to care for me in a tangible way really hit home one night when I was around five. I woke up gasping for air, feeling like I was choking. I managed to run through the house to the only person I knew who could help me: Nonna. If anyone was going to help me it was her, my rock and strength. I could always count on Nonna. I tried as gently as possible to wake her as I did not want to frighten her even though I was so scared myself. Luckily, on her side of the house was a bathroom right beside her bedroom. So as soon as she saw what was happening, she ran with me to the bathroom and turned on the shower to create some steam. She sat me on the floor and got me to breathe deeply. We stayed there until I could breathe properly again. This was to be the first of my many episodes of childhood croup.

Some nights I did not have time to go to the other side of the house to get her, so I would run the shower myself in another bathroom. Once I took a turn for the worst and had to be rushed to hospital. All I remember is wondering why the house lights were still on as we backed down the driveway. It's amazing how the brain filters everything out as that is all I remember of the whole incident. For some reason, I finally grew out of croup when I was about ten.

Other incidents gave me the message that I was pretty much alone. One day I snuck into the kitchen to find the glass bottle of milk in the fridge to give to our cherished pet cat. However, my mother had been doing some washing in the laundry that day and the water in the sink had overflowed. Well, down I went on the floor and sliced my left hand open. I had a 4 x 2 centimetre cut near my thumb, going up to my wrist. This is the time when you really want your mum. However, it wasn't to be.

'Mum, look what I have done!'

Her reply… 'What can I do?'

I have never once blamed her for not helping me as it was just another moment when I had to be self-reliant. I had a considerable wound on my ten-year-old little hand, and blood was everywhere. But Mum just continued washing the clothes.

By this stage I was as white as a ghost. I went to my grandmother and asked for help, but she just told me to go to the retired nurse next door (who happened to be an alcoholic). This was not much help. Luckily that day my brother Sal was at home. I woke him up and he drove me and my grandmother to the hospital. I arrived with just a handkerchief covering my bloodstained hand, which later required seven stiches. I still carry the scar, reminding me every day of how strong I am.

Looking back I never cried once, not when I had fallen, nor at the hospital or afterwards. I just had to do what I had to do. Later in life I would finally shed tears for the little girl who deep down was scared and frightened.

Unwelcome premonitions

While our home had an idyllic Italian backyard, the front was different. We lived on a main arterial road that had three lanes in either direction. With so much traffic came many traffic accidents. There was a crossroad one house up from where we lived, which proved a hazard for anyone attempting to cross the main road. Over time, I realised that I would somehow 'know' a few hours ahead when an accident was going to happen. So I started to play around with this.

I would sit at the front of my house with my faithful dog Ringo and wait for the commotion to take place. It was rare for the ambulance and police not to turn up as the accidents were usually quite bad. On one level I knew that it was destiny and didn't consider I could do anything to prevent what was to happen. So I didn't tell my family.

Seeing mist around me from an early age seemed quite normal too. I honestly thought that everybody could see such things. I was often told 'Get your head out of the clouds and stop being with the fairies,' as whenever they called me, they would have to repeat my name as I would not respond. My mind was elsewhere – often looking up into the sky.

My sister Cecelia and I both used to walk to school with another girl, Antonietta, who lived just down the next street from us. She too came from an Italian family, which always made for some interesting conversations as we could relate to each another. But she and Cecelia finished their schooling before me, which left me eventually walking all alone to and from school. On my walks I often entertained myself with guessing when the lights would change; something I know lots of kids do. But my accuracy was spot on.

Whenever the phone rang, I knew who it was. In the beginning I would just say who it was. 'Ma, Mrs Parisii is calling you!' However, it did not take me long to realise by the expressions on my mother's and grandmother's faces that they clearly did not want me doing this. Maybe I scared them! So I took the hint and stopped telling them. And probably that's why I'd also not say when an accident was about to occur outside.

But I couldn't turn my gift off like a tap. So one day, the phone rang like any other day, but this time I knew the news was not good and my eyes filled with tears. It was the hospital notifying the family that my grandfather Giovanni, Mum's dad, had died. My beautiful grandfather, upon whose knee I used to sit and play games with him , was gone forever. I was 11 and no one said anything to me. No comforting words. Not even a hug. I was not allowed to even go to the funeral.

They thought I was too young. Those were the days when children were expected to not feel or understand, but I felt everything.

I escaped outside to play with my beloved dog Ringo. He was my solace. We had an amazing bond. Then a year later he died, and my heart broke in two. I unfortunately got to witness a council man shovel my most trusted companion into a brown cloth bag and throw him into a garbage truck. The whole situation was handled so cruelly and insensitively by the adults around me. I went to school that day only to return a short time later from becoming violently ill in the stomach. I did not even get a word of condolence or comfort from any member of my family. That's just the way life was. You learned to simply exist. To survive.

The nights were another challenging time for me. I would lie in bed but find it hard to sleep because I could feel so many people in the bedroom. It felt just like when you are attending a function in a room full of people and then shut your eyes. I knew everyone was there but couldn't see them. One night I could not sleep and to my horror I could see a man with a black hat and a coat standing in the corner. I scanned the two windows in my bedroom to see if there was a reflection, but there was none. I was scared. This was the first time I saw a spirit. I knew I couldn't cry out for help to my family. So after what seemed like an eternity, and from sheer exhaustion in trying to stay awake, I eventually fell asleep. In the morning he was gone.

Living with this gift was crazy, but having no one to talk to about it was even worse.

My escape from my insane world was playing the piano and dancing. I was a gifted pianist and talented dancer. Unfortunately, my life came crushing down when my dancing teacher had to move the studio from our suburb. As nobody apart from my dad could drive, there was no way of attending dance classes anymore. The love of my life had been taken from me. Nobody knew how much dance really meant to me as nobody ever asked.

So, at 14, I began to spiral down into depression.

2

Turbulent Teens

The pressure of my family situation and the responsibilities that had been laid upon my shoulders for so many years became too much for me as a teenager. I was struggling to have any free time. In an essentially Italian home, there was no such thing as compromise. All I wanted was to spend time with my friends. I felt like I did not exist. I would often just stay in my room and cry. In fact, I was having a nervous breakdown, but nobody in my family noticed. That is, until I visited my aunty and uncle.

The happiest moments of my childhood were spending school holidays with my Aunty Ann and Uncle Leo in Innisfail in Far North Queensland. I just adored them and loved nothing more than spending time with them and my two cousins, Sam and Josie. I'd fly up on a plane to see them. My aunty had a strong nature and strong intuition, so it did not take long for her to sense on this visit that something was wrong with me. It took an 1800-kilometre journey away from home for someone to see I was not right. In fact, I was broken.

I sat at Aunty Ann's family table and witnessed her on the telephone, giving my father a piece of her mind when she realised my emotional state. No-one had ever stood up for me before like she did. Someone finally saw me; someone stood up for me. Someone could see my pain for the first time.

For just a few weeks I got to experience a new reality. Those short couple of weeks meant the world to me. I was so happy! Riding in the tractor with my cousin was the best, and allowing me to steer the tractor – well, that was *the* best for a city girl like me. We ventured through the sugar cane fields doing checks or any repairs and maintenance that needed to be done. It was awesome! I would fill my lungs with the smell of fresh country air, and of course spend time with the many furry friends that my aunty and uncle owned. I just adored the dogs and cats. But I eventually had to return home. Still, the experience gave me some hope and strength to continue.

Completing my senior year was special considering my family environment. But not before falling down some steps at school one day. I lay on the ground clutching my right foot and rocking like a baby from the pain. My dear close school friend saw me and came to my aid. She helped me up to the head office as that was the protocol. To my astonishment the office lady was having a hard time believing that I had fallen and said I was trying to get out of class. *My god, how ridiculous!* I thought. I felt so angry that she did not believe me. After all, my foot was swollen like a balloon and was turning black and blue. How much more evidence did they need? I limped home, crying with every step.

Arriving home was a relief. There was no chance of going for x-rays or a doctor as my father was away working at sea. Back in those days there was no such thing as internet or mobiles, so the phone directory was all we had. I found the closest chiropractor who just happened to be not far from school. So the next morning I made the slow and painful walk there. After one hour of cold compresses he could finally work on my foot. He proceeded to adjust all the displaced bones in my feet. I screamed with every adjustment. It was a relief for the bones to be finally placed back into order, but my foot was painful and swollen for many months. In fact, it never fully recovered. I just learned to live with it.

Psychic hairdresser

Being the self-reliant person that I am, I managed to complete my schooling without much help from anyone. At times I would try to ask my big sister Cecelia for a hand. But we fought like cats and dogs, as siblings do. We did love each other, of course, and I looked up to her. However, when it came to getting help for schoolwork from her or others in my family, I was pretty much on my own. Not too much was ever accomplished.

At the end of my senior year, I applied for a hairdressing apprenticeship at one of the most sought-after hair salons in Queensland called Stefan Hair Fashions (simply called Stefan's by many). I got accepted. I was so happy! There were hundreds of applicants and only a select few could join this prestigious chain of salons, so I was chuffed. I worked in Stefan's top salon in Brisbane and was trained by some incredible hairdressers. I had a natural talent and flair for the craft. For the first time in my life I started to believe that I had talent.

It was in this environment that I finally got to use my psychic gifts. I had no choice because spiritual stuff started happening. One day, on another busy day in the salon, I was rushed off my feet. My next appointment had just arrived. She was a young lady – no more than 20 years old. Her long, mousey blonde hair fell from her shoulders, and I immediately was captivated by her warm, friendly smile. Something about her presence made me quiver. Within just a few moments, a blinding white light streamed down about one metre away from both of us, touching the left side of her body. My left side vision was gone completely, and I tried desperately to focus and maintain my composure so as not to startle her. At this point I was just so grateful I could still see out of my right eye.

Stay calm. I have to cut this young lady's hair. Who is she? Am I in the presence of an angel in human form?

It took a good 15 minutes to see clearly once again from my left-hand side. I had not experienced anything like this before. A part of me wanted to ask her questions yet I hesitated as I felt her time here on earth was not going to be long and I did not want to scare her with what I saw.

I had fun with my psychic gift, doing countless readings while I was hairdressing. Conveying messages from loved ones and telling clients what was happening in their lives felt so normal. I was like a radio antenna, always open and ready. At this stage of my life I had no real understanding of my gift, and had not yet had the opportunity to speak to someone about mediumship. All I knew was that if I was doing a client's hair and someone who had passed over wanted to deliver a message or let them know that they were okay, I was the messenger, or the go-between.

There are always readings that stand out and somehow leave a lasting impression on me. In all the readings, the Universe does not discriminate when it comes to Spirit wanting to give messages back to loved ones. I have brought through infant babies, murderers, victims of murderers, people who have passed over from all sorts of illness, anorexics, depressed people and suicide victims. As a medium it's so important not to judge the information being given to you.

I remember my first paid reading that I ever did outside of hairdressing. While in the shower the morning of the reading, the message was to give thanks to the young gentleman that shined this elderly man's shoes that he wore in the coffin. I could also see the elderly man shining shoes as well. I received other pieces of information that he was European from Italy (*Of all places*, I thought to myself). Well, it turned out all correct. The young gentleman was his grandson and the elderly man who died shined shoes for a living.

In all the years of doing readings, I don't recall a negative response from anyone. The messages were always well received and the thanks I got were so sincere. It gave me an incredible amount of joy.

Hairdressing at Stefan's was another story. It was a demanding, high-pressure environment, where we had to meet goals and targets set by the company. Lunch was non-existent some days, and even if we were to receive a break it was not until three or four in the afternoon. I became physically and mentally exhausted and could not take much more.

As if the pressure of work was not bad enough, going home every day was worse. It was like entering a battle zone where there was never going to be a winner. My father and I were butting heads. I had grown up right before his eyes, yet he did not see me for who I was. He had also retired too early, and his patience was non-existent. One would think at 19 I would have had some sense of freedom, but this was not the case. In my Italian father's eyes I was still a young girl who had to follow parents' orders.

I considered myself a responsible individual. So one day I rang home to say I was not coming home as I'd had a few drinks at a friend's house and did not want to drive.

The next day I returned home thinking nothing of it. How wrong I was! After opening the glass door to enter home I noticed my mother and grandmother sitting at the kitchen table with the most worried look upon their faces. Before I knew it, my father slapped me across the face. I gasped for air in total shock as he had never laid a hand on me before. The next 15 minutes of my life I endured a spray of spittle from his mouth. Every vile indescribable thing you can hurl at someone was said. Everything changed in a nanosecond. I lost the last slither of respect I had for him. My mother and grandmother said nothing. I said nothing and simply went to my room, in shock.

In that moment, my father had lost all sense of judgement because of his anger and need for control. I now genuinely believe he later regretted his actions. But my dad and I never spoke of that incident, and the worst thing I did was to bury the anger and hurt for nearly 30 years until I finally forgave him.

Meanwhile, my mother was just as sick as she had ever been. Her injuries from the epilepsy seemed to be getting worse. Sometimes I was there in time to see her having a turn just before she would fall. One day I walked into the kitchen and for some reason I looked at my mum and saw that her hand was in the hot frypan just before she fell in front of me. Other times nobody was around and there was a thump and I immediately recognised the sound. My mum had taken another turn and fallen. One day I ran out of my bedroom to find her on the dining room floor with the hot iron on her foot. I was horrified! It was an extremely bad burn, which would ulcerate for many years to come.

My grandmother also was well and truly showing the signs of Alzheimer's. I would find her wandering the house at two in the morning, not knowing what she was doing. I would tell her it was time to sleep and put her back to bed. These nights of broken sleep were taking their toll on me. I was trying to juggle work while caring for my grandmother by showering and dressing her too. Eventually she was placed in a nursing home.

Hitting rock bottom and finding Love

By the time I was in my second year of my apprenticeships as a hairdresser, I felt like my life was a disaster. I couldn't cope any longer. My strength was gone, and I saw no purpose for being here anymore. Finally, one day it all hit me. I felt so alone in the world and simply could not carry the responsibilities on my shoulders anymore. For so long I'd been putting on a smile for everyone to see, but deep down I was in a dark place. I felt dead. I doubted I even deserved a happy life. It seemed like everybody was taking a piece of me. I felt completely worthless and helpless.

Suicide was the only way out.

While I sat on the bed, strategically planning how I was going to end my life, my emotions spiralled downhill even further. Then I suddenly felt a shift. The air around me seemed to change. I felt surrounded by ... love. Love! A bubble of light engulfed me and permeated my being. The hairs on my skin prickled and tears starting streaming down my face as I felt love like I'd never felt before. I could see in my mind's eye, in my head, angelic beings around me, sending the love that I had been so desperately wanting to feel for so long.

It seemed as if the angelic kingdom was on my side. I sensed that they had other plans for me. My plans of suicide were gazumped, ever so lovingly. This moment of divine intervention was to change the course of my life. I was to draw strength from this experience many times in the future. The challenges weren't over yet. But at least I knew I was loved, and such love it was!

There were many more challenging times in the years to follow. Amidst those moments I still loved my father and deep down I knew I was loved by him. It was a changing time for both of us.

Six months after having my twenty-first, I lost my third grandparent, my father's mother, Nonna Capri. I volunteered to do the prayers at the funeral service. Somebody had to do it, so I thought it was my way of contributing to her send-off. I walked slowly up to the podium to read the prayers, trying to keep my emotions together. I was not even halfway through the first prayer and broke down in tears, which started off a wave of crying throughout the entire congregation. But in a way I wasn't crying from grief. I was overwhelmed with my tremendous love for my grandmother and her love for me, as I could feel her arm around me from behind. Once again, I could feel that love surrounding me. I knew what it felt like; it was her.

I continued reciting those prayers through my tears. Looking back, I don't know how I finished all those prayers. But there was one thing I did know, and that was that love never dies.

Learning my lesson the hard way

I eventually became a fully qualified hairdresser, something I was immensely proud of as it had been a tough four years. Just shy of my twenty-second birthday, I embarked on my first overseas holiday to America, Canada and Hawaii. I'd been saving up over the previous year and had quit my job at Stefan's to travel. It was on the very last leg of my stay in America that I was to learn the hard way about listening to your feelings.

While staying at the Hyatt in Hollywood, Los Angeles, I found out that a famous American singer, Little Richard, was living in the adjacent hotel room, with his bodyguards occupying a room across the hallway. I had the opportunity to meet him, which was exciting. I wanted to see the sights of Los Angeles as I had allocated a week in the area, so I hired a car and asked one of the bodyguards to show me around. It was an amazing week, but all good things come to an end and I had to return the car.

I had arranged for the hire company to collect the car from where I was staying. But the 'gentleman' who had been driving me around said that he would return the car for me. *Oh, what a nice guy!* I thought. As I sat on the bed to make the call to the hire company to change plans, I suddenly felt like my insides were turned upside down. I had a terrible sick feeling all over. *Strange…* But I didn't stop to listen in.

Then two weeks after returning home to Australia, I received a phone call and was shocked to hear that the car had not been returned. The man had stolen it! I was horrified! I learned that the car hire company had been billing me for the hire of the car all this time, and they were not going to stop until the car was returned. I felt so helpless. I went through weeks of heartache. I was challenged mentally, emotionally and financially.

On reflection, I realised I hadn't listened to that sick feeling in my gut when I decided to let the bodyguard return the car. It was a psychic message. This was a profound lesson to listen in and to have faith. Only the week before I'd read about how you must have faith and trust that your prayers are answered. So now I was certainly praying for help out of this predicament. My cries for help were indeed answered when I found a top law firm in Brisbane who got the car hire company to stop debiting my account. And then my father bailed me out financially to pay off the rest of my credit card, for which I was ever so grateful. Finally, the Los Angeles police found the car and the guy went to court.

Through this whole experience I knew that to survive in this world, I would have to learn to trust the messages I receive. And I was determined to do that. Trust and have faith. I sent a little prayer up that I could be shown how to develop my gifts, and promised that I would use them wisely from now on.

Well, soon it became clear that that prayer was going to be answered.

3

My Learning Begins

You don't know who your neighbours truly are until you really get to know them. I was in my early twenties and living on the Gold Coast and had to give my neighbour across the road some money as her son had recently mowed our lawn. Well, how lucky was I! It turned out that this lady was one of the most spiritual ladies I was to ever meet. And she was unofficially to become my first spiritual teacher.

Her name was Gay. During that first visit to Gay's house, my dear deceased grandmother decided to make her presence known. Gay turned to me and started describing my grandmother, simply saying, 'Your grandmother has been trying to get your attention for a long time'.

I was ecstatic! My father's mother had only died a few years before. This was so exciting! It was the first time someone else was doing a reading for me. Gay could see and hear my Nonna Angela. You know the old saying, 'When the student is ready, the teacher will come.' Gay was my ray of sunshine. Finally, someone I could talk to with knowledge in metaphysical topics.

I became Gay's student. From then on, we spoke often on numerology, astrology, spiritual masters, crystals and much, much more. She was 15 years my senior and had much more knowledge than me, so I was like a sponge, asking question after question. Whatever I needed to know she just seemed to have the answer.

Developing my gifts

I began keeping diaries and writing all that I learned. I wrote down everything that happened to me: my dreams, premonitions and all the quirky spiritual things that occurred daily. This helped me understand the knowledge and spiritual growth I had been experiencing. This was my development. I never attended any classes or groups. This was my learning – the start of my passion.

I was in love with learning and began reading books. I wanted to know more about myself, my gift and the non-physical. I was 100 percent committed. My inquisitiveness was my driving force. Every time I learnt something was just a drop in the ocean; there was more to learn. I was on a mission. I began to understand what my spiritual gifts were and how to use them.

Every time I am given a message, I become the receiver as well. Being a channel medium I am tuning into higher frequencies. I feel I am the lucky one as I can feel these energies through me. Every medium will tell you their own way of receiving messages. I will give you an insight as to what happens with me. My insights arrive in a variety of ways.

First, I have been gifted with inner sight – clairvoyance. I would describe this as like a television set in my brain where I am able to see another reality as clear as day. I am using my physical body, my eyes and brain, as well as my non-physical sight and mind. There is like an overlap of the two. One exists with the other.

The other experience I have is that I feel like there is an energy of electricity around me and I have the sensation of having a set of false teeth in my mouth. I am placed somewhat in a daydream; you could say I am focused elsewhere.

I also have clairsentience, where I can feel a message sent via the emotions. For example, if someone has a vibrant personality and is funny, I can feel the personality, and this goes for the other extreme. Sometimes the contact may wish to show me what they have been feeling during their time on Earth. Be it sadness or loneliness, I get to experience this as well.

When love is sent to clients, I receive it first, and sometimes quite intensely. I do not know when it is going to happen, so when it does it's quite overwhelming. I can be in tears from the love I feel being sent by the other side. I had to learn to mentally pass this feeling on to the client for them to receive. I do not really know when I started referring to the spirits as 'the other side', but it stuck with me and it's an easy way to refer to non-physical beings.

I can also remote view, where I can see where you wish to see without being there.

As a child it was a little confusing having all these gifts that I couldn't talk about with anyone else. So please, if your child happens to mention that they can see or hear spirits, don't dismiss them. Show them photos of loved ones as they may have seen your parent or grandparent or someone else you may know. Children have just come from the other side and are more open to receive spirits.

Some of the children that have been coming to Earth have been given special gifts more highly advanced than you can ever imagine. I am not only talking about seeing and hearing spirits and having healing abilities. I am also referring to knowing and remembering their past lives and knowing galactic connections. They do not have to be told certain information because they already know. Their higher thinking is more evolved. The way they see the world is different. Embrace these beautiful souls for they are the future, and many have come here to help heal the world. They bring with them new discoveries and new inventions. Allow them to flourish and to be their authentic selves, for the world needs change and they come to help.

Men and bambinos

While my spiritual learning was expanding, my personal relationships were problematic. I mostly attracted men with alcohol or drugs problems. I seemed to accept any form of love. I was searching for acceptance and wanting to fit in. This acceptance was possibly an escape. In short, I experienced infidelity, verbal abuse and a degree of physical abuse from these men. Finally, at 25 my luck seemed to turn.

I met a guy at Sea World on the Gold Coast where I worked, and I fell in love with him. He was originally from another state, New South Wales, and intended to go back to his hometown at Tahmoor. His mum was living in the adjoining town of Bargo, a small town 100 kilometres south of Sydney. I decided to follow him back to Bargo and we got engaged. We married and would spend the next 18 years together.

By the time we had the first of our three beautiful children, the cracks in our marriage were appearing. Yet I threw myself into trying to be the perfect wife and mother and ignored what was really going on. I would keep myself extremely busy, like cleaning the house even when it did not need doing. This I would call my 'nervous energy'.

My children became my world, my heart and soul, and everything I did was always for them. I would always stand up and protect them no matter what the situation was. I wanted to give them the childhood that I never got. Their schooling was so important as I did not want them to go through the struggles that I went through. I was involved in every aspect of their lives as this gave me so much joy. I loved being a mum! I was so enormously proud of all their achievements, and I felt I was there to support them and help them fulfil whatever their wishes were.

I also tried to be the best daughter-in-law and became my mother-in-law's carer. I helped to take care of her through ten major operations. We shared a close bond and countless cups of tea together. She was a loving grandmother to the children.

Looking back over those years, I can see that I seemed to lose my own identity. In doing so much for others I never gave myself the respect I deserved. I suppose I felt that I'd never received it, and as a child I just did so much for my family. You don't realise how you give your power away and allow manipulation and control to easily slip into your life without you knowing it. I had been controlled my entire life and I did not yet know anything different. This relationship was certainly no different. I had to break free of shackles, figuratively speaking, and take responsibility for my own actions.

I had allowed others to tell me what to do for too long. I taught others how to treat me, always putting myself second best and never thinking I deserved anything. I loved my children unconditionally, yet I did not think I deserved the love myself.

I ultimately felt broken, merely existing. I wasn't living. You can see a clear blue sky but not appreciate it if you are not present in the moment.

Ciao Nonna and Mamma

While living interstate, I would return home back to Brisbane every year to visit my family. One visit was unforgettable. Prior to returning home I would often dream of my Nonna Maria. But this time it was more than just a dream. She said to me, 'The next time you visit I will see you'. I thought this strange as my grandmother had full-blown Alzheimer's and had not opened her eyes in a long time. She was totally bedridden and required nursing staff to move her.

I went to the nursing home like every other visit and sat down beside her. 'Nonna, I am here.' Well, she sat straight up in bed, looked at me, nodded, opened her eyes, smiled and lay back down! The whole moment would have lasted but ten seconds. I totally freaked out, ran out the room and went straight to the nurse station, babbling my words so incoherently I don't think even I understood what I was saying. I was in total shock over what I had just witnessed.

I know that what I experienced was true. I believe that for a moment it defied all logic. The nurses calmly said to me, 'Your grandmother could not have done that as we have to lift and move her'.

Well, there are some things that words cannot explain, but I know that what I had witnessed. It was true even though it defied all physical abilities of my grandmother at that time.

When my grandmother finally passed over a couple of years later, I mourned her leaving and remembered her unconditional love for me. She'd raised me as a little girl, and as sad as I was, I knew it was a blessing for she was free and no longer trapped in her body.

My mother's passing was quite different. My father, brother, sister and I were able to be with her when she took her final breath and passed over. It was a privilege. Five days beforehand, I'd sat down beside her bed and asked her if she could give me a sign when she passed over, and she was true to her word. The air in the room changed and I felt spirits walking from behind me, coming to meet her. I was standing by her bed with the palm of my hand placed alongside her body. In her final breath, wind moved up my arm to my elbow as I felt her beautiful soul leave her body. At the same time, I yet again experienced that unconditional love exploding in every cell in my body.

I immediately asked the family, 'Did you feel it?' But they didn't understand what I was talking about. The experience was a gift from my mum to me alone, and now I can share it with you.

Other dimensions

In my mid-thirties I just had to write! The urge wouldn't go away. Sometimes I would write notes from a book I had read. At other times, in moments of stillness I would hear the words in my mind and had to write them down. I never knew what I was going to write as it would be in the moment, somewhat like dictation. This was to be the beginning of recommitting to my spiritual learning and growth.

One day, this stream of consciousness flowed out:

Two worlds are joined as one, blended like interwoven threads of fabric, endless through the worlds of space, time and matter.
It just exists; the world was formed to show matter of its existence.
A state of being and its matter.
You see the two are the same. Same threads, some visible using physical senses, some are not.
There is so much hatred and so much crime. It does not matter, for love will conquer all and will prevail over darkness and good will combat the evil.
When we learn we progress.
So you see, what you see has always a hidden agenda and a purpose.
Sometimes the world does not look hard enough to see what has been taught.
They only see the physical being and not the other side.
It is only when we start to look at things with two eyes at both sides that we truly see.

Not long after writing this I went to sit in the lounge for some quiet time to contemplate what I had just written. I had read countless books up until this stage, and at 35 I thought there was something missing. That day I worked out that all the books I had read had one common denominator: *their authors had demonstrated an inner knowing that to their teachings.* My attitude had been that I had to find something outside of myself. That day, on the couch, I had an epiphany. Such an obvious one now, I shake my head:

The answers have been within me all along.

I had to go within and trust myself. That was the key. I had to stop using my physical eyes and start using my inner sight to see.

So I sat there on the lounge in a kind of daydream and then, after a short time, my eyes could see the auras of everything in the room. There was not one piece of furniture that did not have a white light. What I was seeing was pulsating as I tried to adjust my eyes. After a while I just gave up, relaxed and let myself go.

My eyes were still open, and the room started to disappear. Everything that was around me no longer took form; everything disappeared. At this point I could have freaked out, but I remained calm, fascination and curiosity taking hold. The array of colours was beautiful, and I could make out shadows of people walking by. It was peaceful. I think I was just shocked that I could not see the room anymore. My attention was in this amazing space that I never knew existed until now.

At this time I had no idea what I had experienced, but I knew it was real. I truly had an experience of going within.

After this I began a practice of writing a question and receiving an answer, even more confident to know that the answers were within me already. In 2009 I wrote, 'I want to be inspired. What is my purpose?' And this is what came to me. The transcript has not been changed:

It is to create each moment.
Every second of your human existence, don't waste time for it is precious. Become conscious of every moment.
Cherish your human existence.

Make a list of all the things you want to experience and feel.

Feel your experience. It allows God to feel.

Do not look at things as right or wrong. Do not judge what others will do or not do. Do not be concerned with other people's thoughts.

You have an incredibly unique view of the world, as individual as every snowflake, every cloud formation.

You truly live when you live without fear and live with freedom. THE TRUTH WILL SET YOU FREE.

It's all about the experience of the Creation.

Money does not give you all the joyous experiences. It will help you create some but not all.

You must find balance.

It's good to acknowledge what you feel, to be conscious of your feelings. Choose to feel the world and how you want to feel.

Love unconditionally, love all equally, bless everyone. Acknowledge the goodness in everything and everything that has been – because it is all God.

I read this piece of writing over and over during the following weeks. It was like someone was trying to give me clues and meaning to life. I never imagined that these words written back in 2009 would be shared with you now. There was much more learning that I had to experience and my thirst for knowledge was growing at an exponential rate. Somehow, I knew that I was putting the puzzle pieces together, joining the dots and making connections.

The week I wrote the above passage turned out to be an incredibly special week. My beloved mum who had passed away one year earlier decided to pay me a visit from Spirit World. I had so much trouble falling asleep, and this night I kept seeing vivid white mist floating in the room. It wouldn't go away, and after an exhausting couple of hours of restlessness, I finally dozed off.

When someone has passed over, one form of communication occurs when we sleep. While asleep, our conscious awareness is no longer directed to the physical state but our true spiritual self. Sometime during the night, I became very conscious within my dream state. I was standing in the kitchen of the house I grew up in and my beautiful mum was standing with her face turned side-on to me. I immediately recognised her and told her, 'Mum, please turn around. I want to see you.' She was reluctant at first but then turned to me. I was so happy! She looked so young and not sick anymore.

'I was tired and did not want to stay any longer on Earth,' she said.

I told her it was okay. I was just excited to see her.

She then told me, 'I will be waiting for Dad when he comes.' She had to go.

'I miss you and I don't want you to go,' I pleaded.

In that moment I experienced the same beautiful feeling of love exploding through every cell of my body again, just like I felt at her bedside when she passed away. I awoke with tears streaming down my face and the realisation that I had not finished grieving her loss. Grabbing a blanket, I went into the lounge room and curled up like a baby as I continued to cry and release all my pain.

4

Contact

14.9.2011

By the time I was 40 we had relocated back to the Gold Coast. My continuing journey of spiritual awareness was to take a quantum leap while the cracks in my marriage became wider and wider. It was as if on one hand I was stepping up and on the other I was falling.

In September 2011, my husband and children went back to Bargo to visit family and friends without me as I had to work. About 10 pm on the 14th (I noted all these dates and in time the dates and numbers proved significant.), I was feeling very tired and went to bed, looking forward to a good night's sleep.

Fluffing my pillow, I finally laid my head to rest and closed my eyes. But not for long. After only about 20 seconds, I had an overwhelming feeling to open my eyes. Well! Still laying on my bed and wide awake, I was astonished to see a structure four metres wide spanning across my whole bedroom, from wall to wall.

It was about two metres high and just within arm's reach. The central structure was about one metre by one metre with triangles within triangles moving and changing with more complexity than any computerised image. There were two beings on either side of this central structure. They were not as clearly defined as the structure. Nevertheless I could see the outline of their heads and shoulders. I desperately tried to focus to get a clearer picture of their faces, but it was as if they were faded out. This magnificent holographic triangular structure was a deep sea-blue colour mixed with a deep purple. It was beautiful! The outer perimeter of the whole structure was smooth and moving like it was under water.

It was multidimensional, appearing solid yet I could see through it. I had to test to see what it felt like, so I lifted my hand, and it went right through! You would think I'd be afraid, but I wasn't. Instead I experienced a sense of peace, love and calmness. Suddenly the back window and wall behind my bed disappeared and was replaced with a blinding white light. All I could say was 'WOW, WOW and WOW!'

This entire experience defied all human logic as to time and space. I was fully present in the physical and awake, yet I was also in the presence of beings from another dimension. They stayed with me for a couple of minutes, as if they wanted me to never forget their visitation. I was mesmerised and knew this was real and alive.

The whole encounter had an energy of its own.

I lay in bed and recalled the whole event that had just taken place, thinking that this had to have been one of the coolest, most extraordinary experiences I had ever had. My world had taken on a whole new dimension, literally.

My life was never going to be the same again. I had just made my first contact. Who were these beings and what were they showing me? I now had questions that needed to be answered. One way or another I had to learn more. This was the first of many encounters.

The next morning I could not wait to tell my friend June as I knew she would not think I was crazy. She was a Reiki Healing Master. I'm quite sure that my visit with her the day before –the day of my visitation – was no coincidence. She had done a Reiki healing on me. For those who may not know, Reiki is a healing modality where a Reiki practitioner channels high frequency energy into someone else through touch. This activates the natural healing processes within the recipient to restore physical and emotional balance. The recipient can release emotions and clear blockages that may otherwise be holding them back, for example, letting go of painful experiences.

June said that she had seen in her mind's eye my kundalini awakening. This means a quickening of the energy chakras in the body. I certainly did receive a spiritual awakening; that night proved it for me. This experience was just the start for there was more to come, much more.

The drawings begin

30.9.2011 A special design

On the last day of September in 2011, I received a message from Spirit to purchase some chalk and paper. I had never used chalk before but instinctively knew I was to draw. But what? By then I had learnt to trust my messages, and this one came with a sense of urgency, so I did not waste any time.

That very night at exactly 9.11 pm, I sat on the floor beside my bed and breathed deeply for about a minute, just relaxing and bringing my attention to outside of myself. Very soon I noticed about one inch above the white piece of paper a yellow cobweb design beginning to present itself from the top of the page and forming all the way down the page. It stayed there for about 10 seconds and then disappeared. I could not believe my eyes! I had never seen this before. I took it as a sign to commence drawing. I had no idea what I was about to draw; nevertheless, I just had to trust in whatever was guiding me.

I felt like I was in a daydream. I put the chalk to the page and began drawing triangles within triangles. Somehow, they all had a specific placement and size on the page. I knew it had a meaning, but I had no idea at this stage what that was. When the drawing was completed, I felt myself return to the conscious state. At the same time some energy lifted off me, which caused the hair on my skin to react.

The next morning I eagerly showed my drawing to June to see if she could shed some light on the matter. She told me several different meanings that she believed they could be associated with. I realised that I had so much to learn, which fuelled my fascination even more.

This first picture would be one of the most significant drawings for me as it would become the emblem for my website Kosmic Connections, which would come some nine years later.

After this more drawings occurred. They would come naturally and without expectations. Nearly all drawings were done freehand and would take anywhere from 30 minutes to one hour depending on the details of the picture. Every drawing was done at 9.11 or 11.09 am or pm, which when added up numerologically, always came to 11.

30.9.2011 Drawing #1

12.12. 2011 The Messenger

Over time, I channelled four more drawings of faces of different beings: a Pleiadean (beings from Pleiades), a Blue Man, Bashar from the Essene people and a Star Being. I believe the purpose of these drawings was to show me that the ETs could be so different in shape and form, and that they were in some way connected to me.

Then there were spaceship drawings, which were just so amazing! The shapes and sizes were so different. One picture was of a mothership, meaning it was a carrier of other spaceships, a headquarters or command station. Other pictures would only show sections of the crafts. Later I would come across real footage of the exact spaceships I had drawn. And this would give me incredible conformation that what I had drawn was real.

With each drawing I would draw and rub out continually until I finally felt it was right. Sometimes when I had finished the drawing, I automatically had knowledge about the drawing. Once I asked why I had so much trouble drawing a picture and I was told that human minds and DNA were changing. Our two strand DNA was changing, and the non-physical DNA strands were being activated. Just like a flower represents life and opens, we too are changing, and this activation is different for everyone. Eventually everyone will awaken. Those who make the transition to the Spirit World will continue to awaken there. No one is left behind.

12.12.2011 Drawing #2 'The Messenger'

22.12.2011 Drawing #3

23.12.2011 Drawing #4

24.12.2011 Drawing #5

My ET experiences continue

25.12.2011 Akashic Record and tears

A couple of months after my first drawings, I had another multi-dimensional experience. Once again, I was lying in bed ready for a good night's sleep. I had just closed my eyes for a short time when I instinctively opened them. Hovering above my body was a gold book emanating a golden light that flooded most of the room. I immediately knew what it was: an Akashic Record book. Akashic Records are recorded information of all human events. Your thoughts, words, emotions and even intentions in the past, present or future are recorded in your own Akashic Record book. I would call it a written manuscript in the non-physical plane.

The book I saw would have been half a metre wide by half a metre tall and was hovering above my body. The book was open and had writing on the pages, but it was not written in English. There was a beam of light from the book to my body, and even though I could not read the writings I could feel the book even though it was holographic.

I wasn't sure why I was seeing the book. I presumed it was my own Akashic Record Book. But soon I would know. My world was about to be turned upside down.

***

The next morning began the most intense spiritual cleansing that my body and soul had ever experienced. It lasted for four days. From the moment I rose out of bed, tears just poured out. The book seemed to be giving me access to my whole life. I could feel waves of energy coming from within me *and* coming towards my body. My mind could visibly see the pain and trauma of all my life experiences right in front of me, as one picture after another flashed up, almost like on a movie screen. I cried nonstop.

After the first few hours I was saying out loud to the space around me, 'No more! I cannot do this'. I just wanted the tears and emotional pain to stop. And as if someone had heard, I experienced moments of not feeling anything for about one minute. Then it would start all over again. I would eventually fall sleep from just sheer exhaustion.

Then when awake it would begin again. I would be recalling and feeling the past with such clarity! I had total understanding of the experiences; I understood why I underwent the physical emotions of pain and I learned where I had not previously learned from the experiences. I could also see the role of all those who interacted with me in co-creating those experiences. I was also releasing all the unconscious fear I was carrying, and the unconscious beliefs that I been taught or picked up along the way. Every fear-based belief was stripped from the depths of my being. I purged all those unexpressed emotions, from a little girl right up to my current age. I released in tears everything that no longer served me, until there was nothing left to release. Tears serve a purpose. They are the by-product of the chemical reaction that takes place within your body in the letting go of what no longer serves you.

After those days came an inner stillness. I had emptied everything out, and I did not know who I was anymore. Nothing was the same. Everything around me felt foreign. I felt like the hard drive of a computer that has just been wiped clean.

At the end of these four days I made an important decision: I was going to leave my husband.

I knew I was not happy. I had to have faith that everything was going to be alright. All I wanted was for my kids to be okay with what I was about to do. The moment of power for me was finally deciding that the marriage was not for me and not to feel guilty about my decision. This was my decision for myself and no-one else.

There had been so many things about myself that I had not been expressing. Not being genuinely me. I was not expressing who I truly was. It was time to give myself the freedom and space to finally be the real me. Time to start living differently. I had allowed the wishes of others dictate to me who and what I should be for too long, ultimately putting my spiritual needs aside.

31.12.2011 Time of transformation

A few days later, I had another one of those amazing multi-dimensional experiences. I was lying awake in my pitch-black bedroom and saw up in the air something slowly appearing. A magnificent gold flower was moving as if sprouting for the first time. It was about one metre wide by one metre high. This was accompanied by different faces forming and disappearing beside the flower, surrounded by glowing white balls of light. By this time I had grown accustomed to these experiences. Still I was amazed by its structure and how it was moving and appeared so alive.

I now see that this flower was representing my life. Everything in life changes; we experience life, and we experience death. My release of emotions only a week before was the dying and letting go of everything that no longer served me, and this flower was representing the new. I understood the faces as being the many faces that we show the world. This was my transformation into someone new. Deep down I wanted change, but I did not know how. I was a clean slate, and everything was going to be new. I was creating a new life and with this process also came the unknown. I had to have trust and faith in this force that was guiding me.

My decision was final. My husband and I would separate. We were very amicable in the decision, splitting everything evenly, including our time with our children. We both loved our children unconditionally.

While my physical family was splitting, my spiritual self was opening up exponentially.

For the next four months, spaceship after spaceship began appearing to me, all sorts of shapes and sizes. And the drawings kept happening. Every drawing continued to be done at 9.11 or 11.09 am or pm.

24.4.2012 An unexpected visitation

On the night of 24th April 2012, I found myself drawing a human being. When I drew a crown across his forehead, I knew who it was! It was Jesus! A huge wave of emotions welled up and exploded within me. Tears flowed freely, wetting the paper on the floor. They were tears of love. How on earth was I to finish this picture?

I went and got a towel, and as I desperately mopped up the tear blotches, I had a sudden sense of deja vu...

I remembered a connection with Jesus I had as a little girl. Every time I had sat and watched a movie that Jesus was depicted in, I would cry. I never knew why I did this. And here I was, a fully grown adult and crying again. But this time I understood

Christ consciousness would be awakened in us all.

more. This was a particularly important picture indeed. Without going into the subject of religion too much, I understood what it represented: the second coming of Christ. But not in the sense that Jesus would come in the physical again but rather that the Christ consciousness would be awakened in us all.

Jesus' origins were not of Earth, but we are no different to he who walked on Earth many years ago in that he did not need to follow anyone. He already knew who he was. We all must find that Christ consciousness within us as our connection to Creation. Jesus needed to become aware of his Christhood, so must we. This is what the second coming means. It is the wave of conscious awakening within all humans.

22.4.2012 Drawing #22

5.1.2012 Drawing #6

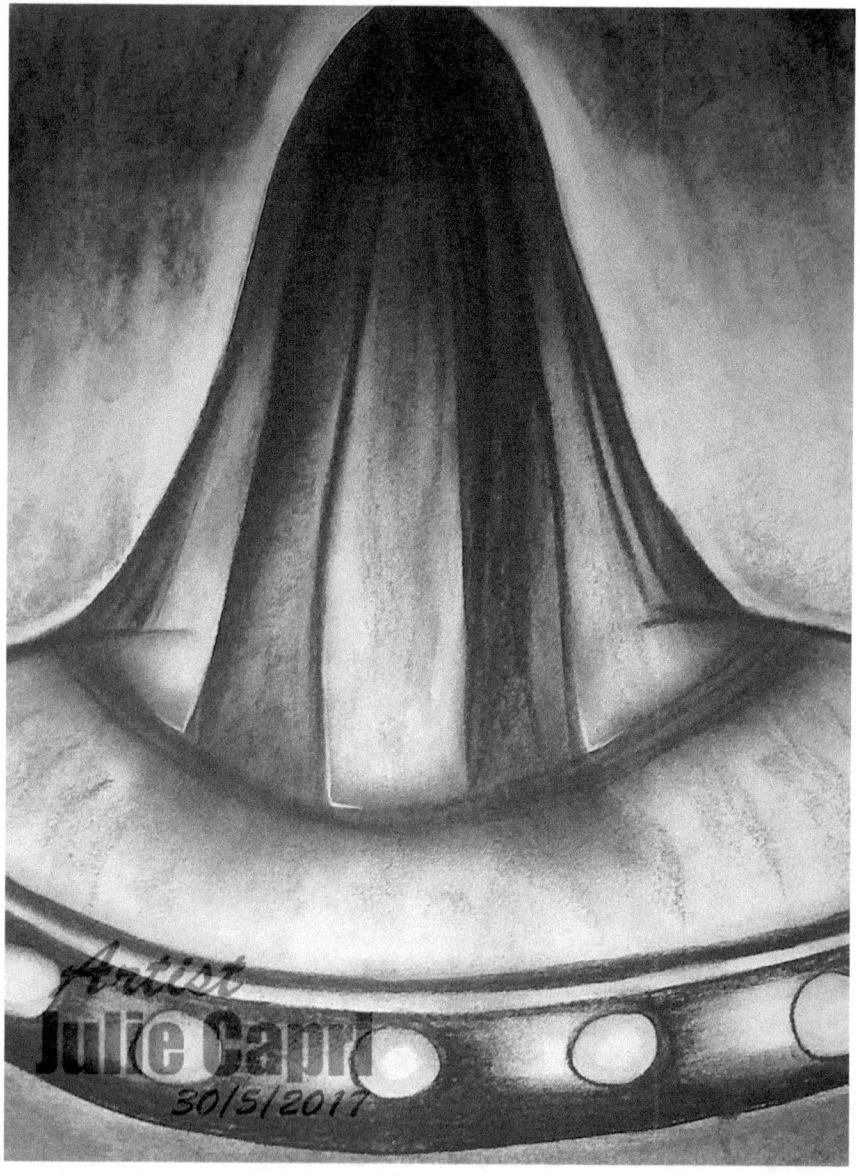

9.1.2012 Drawing #7

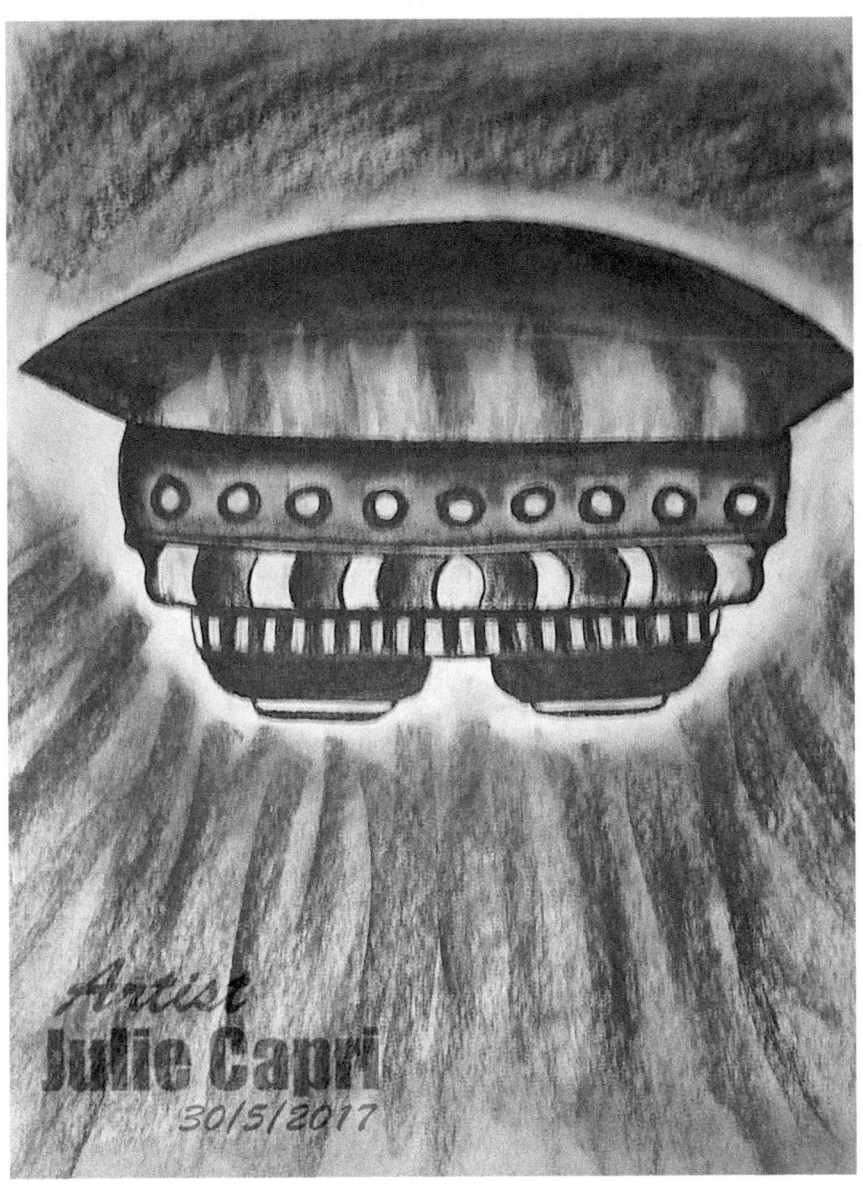

24.1.2012 Drawing #8

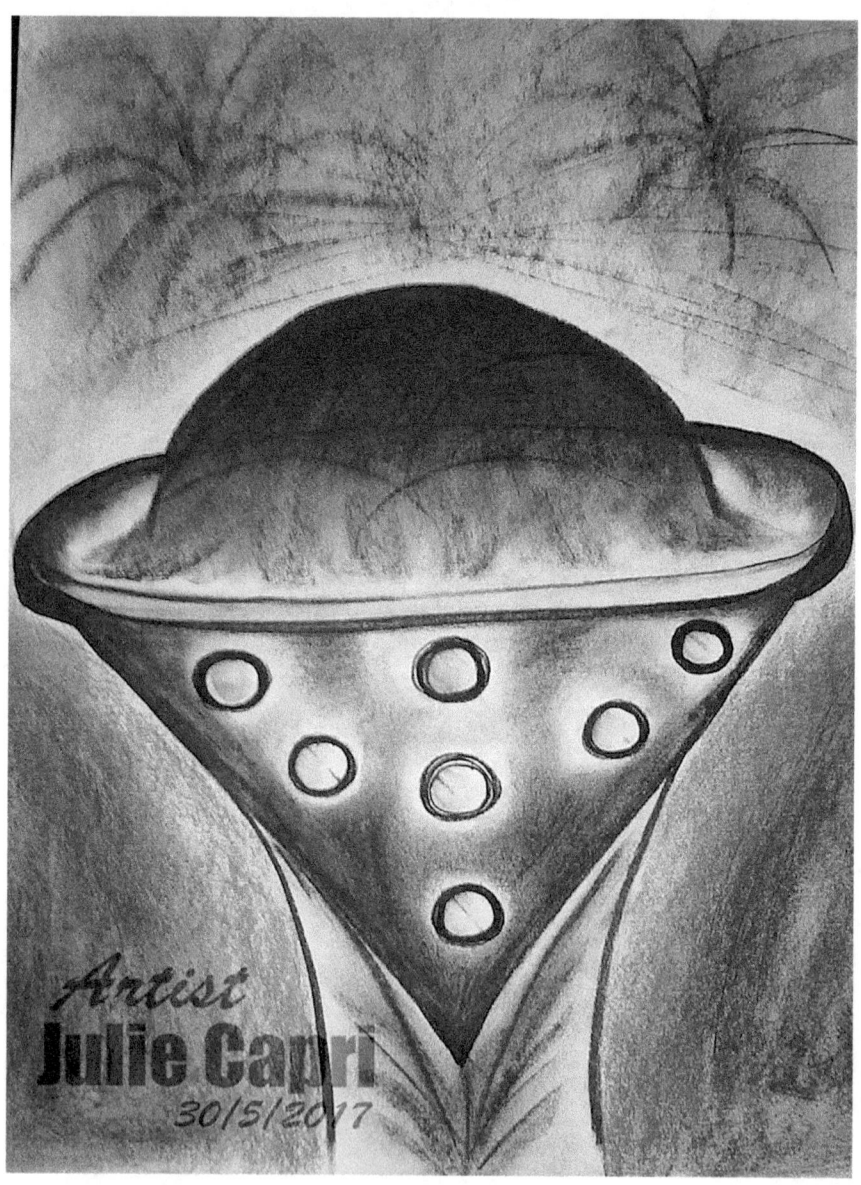

25.1.2012 Drawing #9

30.1.2012 Drawing #10

Awakening: It's time to remember who you really are

31.1.2012 Drawing #11

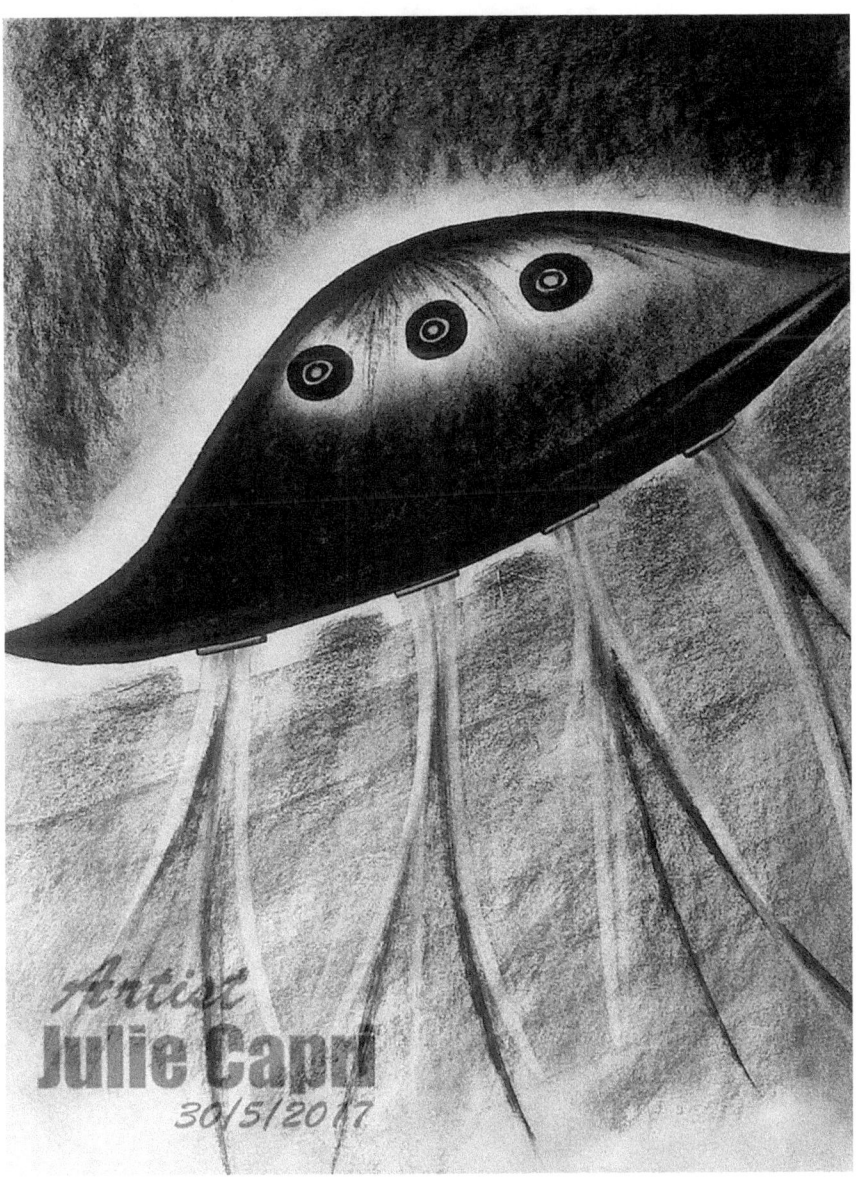

45

5.2.2012 Drawing #12

6.2.2012 Drawing #13

11.2.2012 Drawing #14

13.2.2012 Drawing #15

21.2.2012 Drawing #16

Awakening: It's time to remember who you really are

29.2.2012 Drawing #17

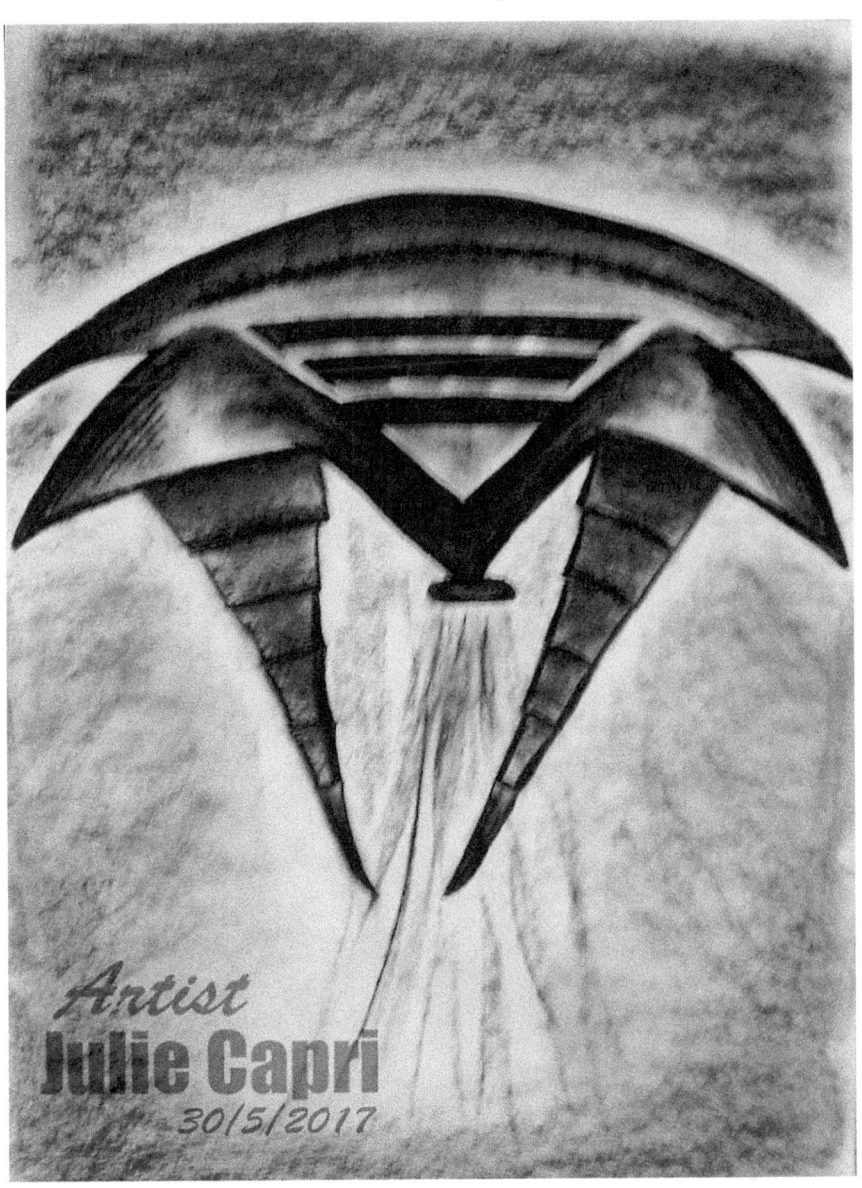

13.3.2012 Drawing #18

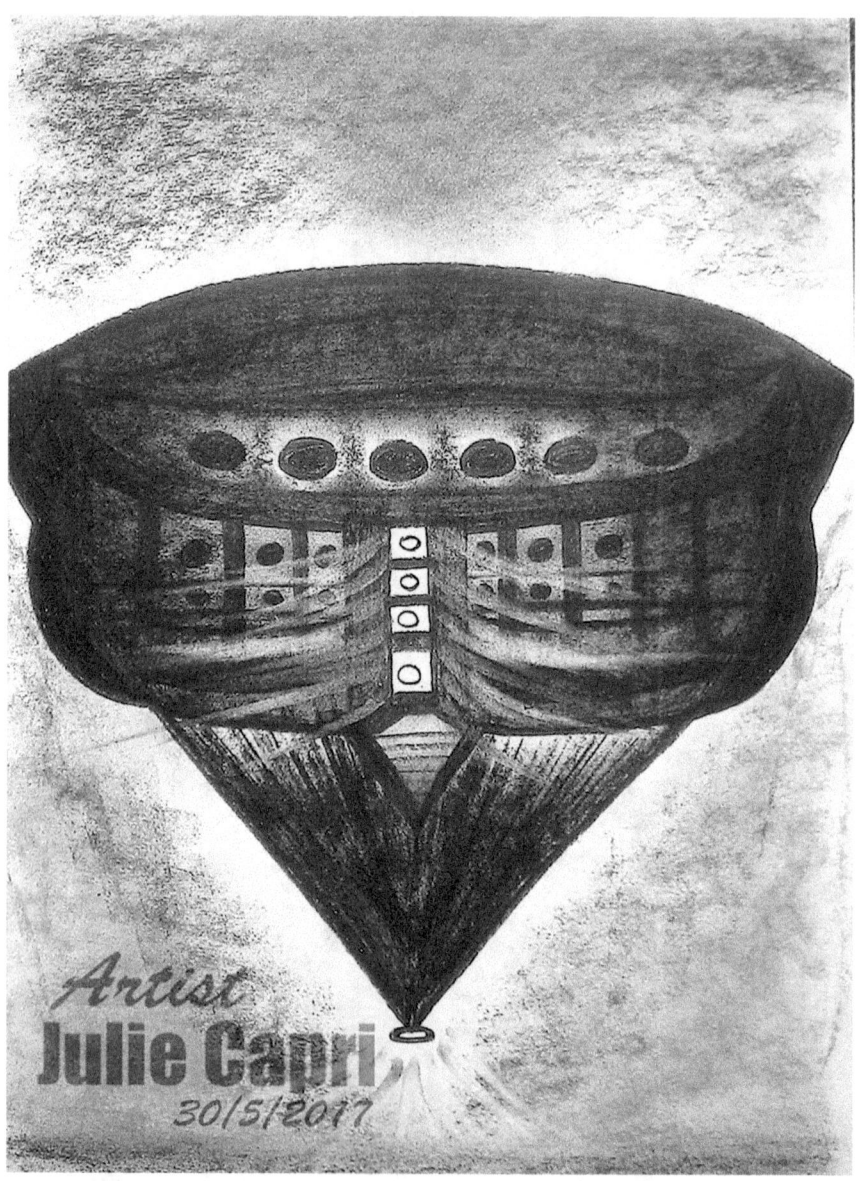

14.3.2012 Drawing #19

20.3.2012 Drawing #20

17.4.2012 Drawing #21

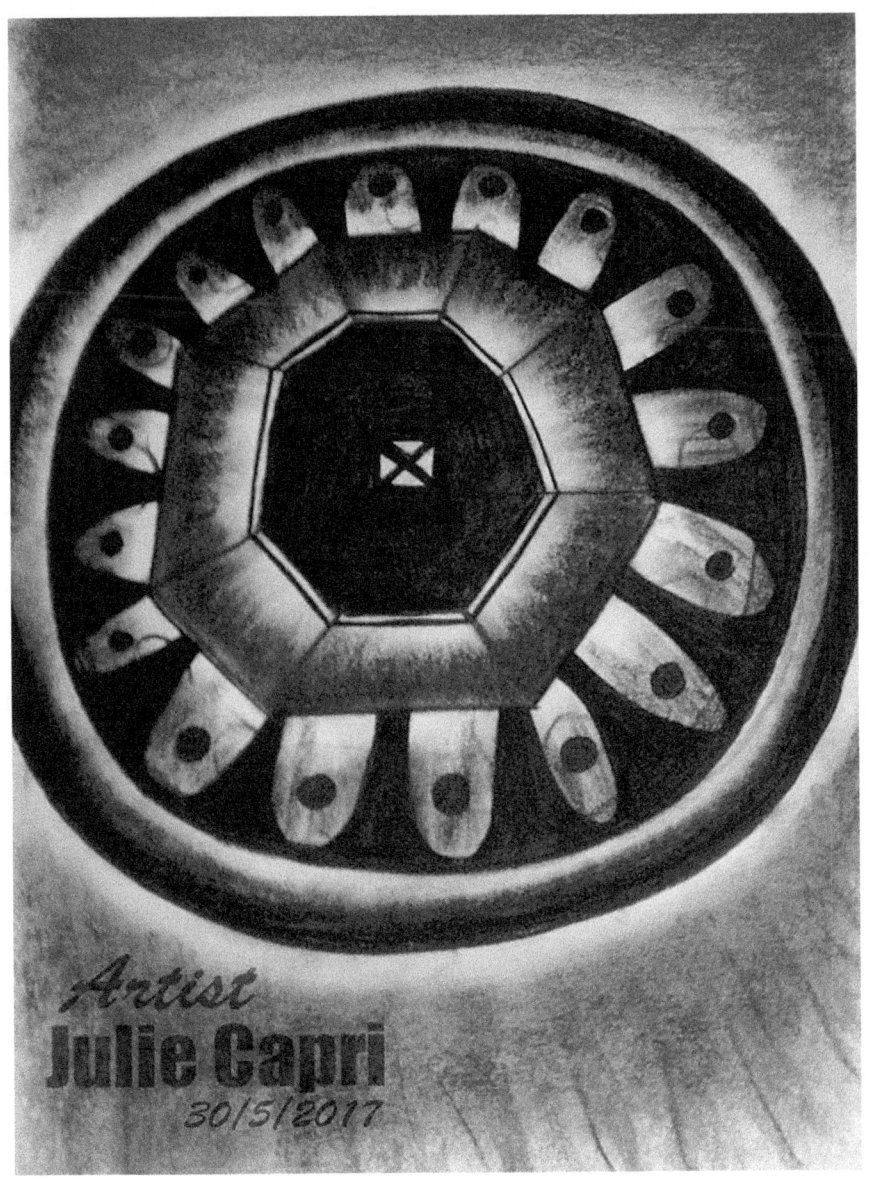

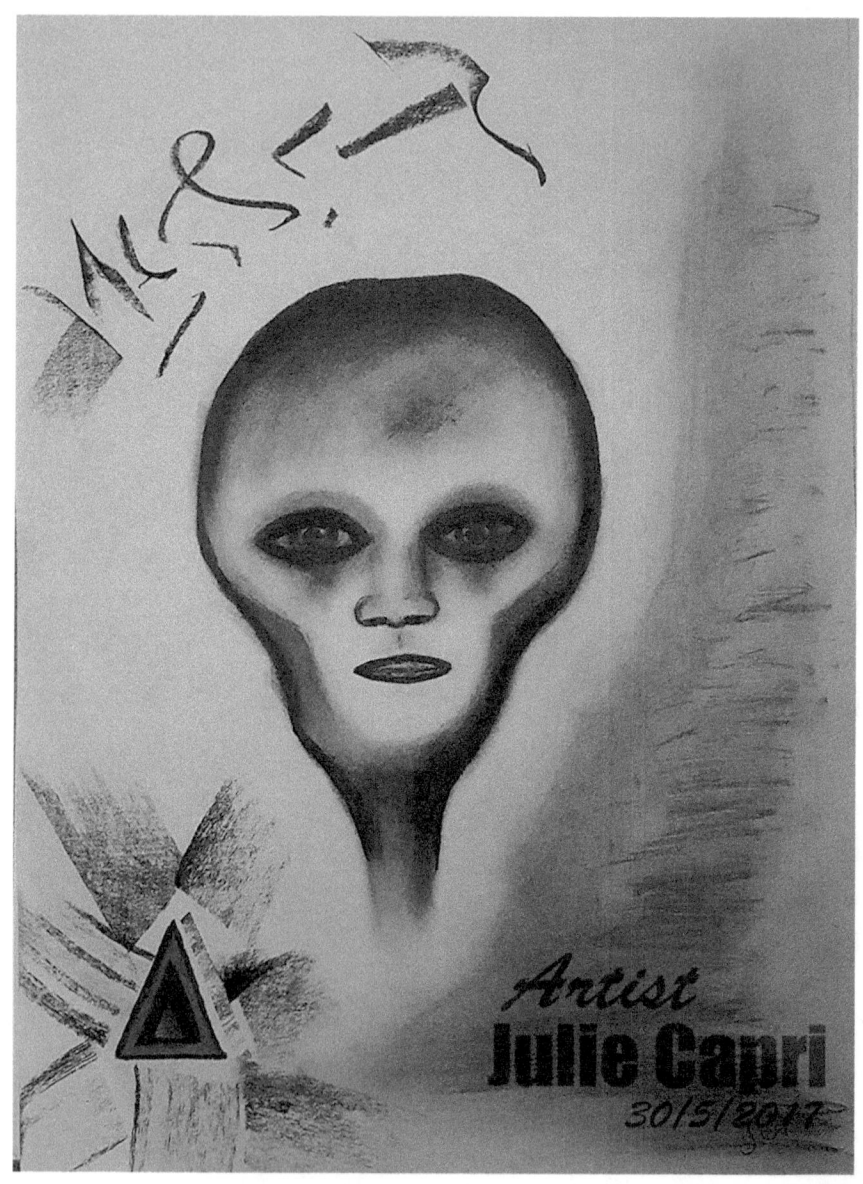

4.5.2012 Drawing #23

6.6.2012 Drawing #24

6.6.2012 Drawing #25 Two-Strand DNA changing

12.7.2012 Drawing #26 Blue alien

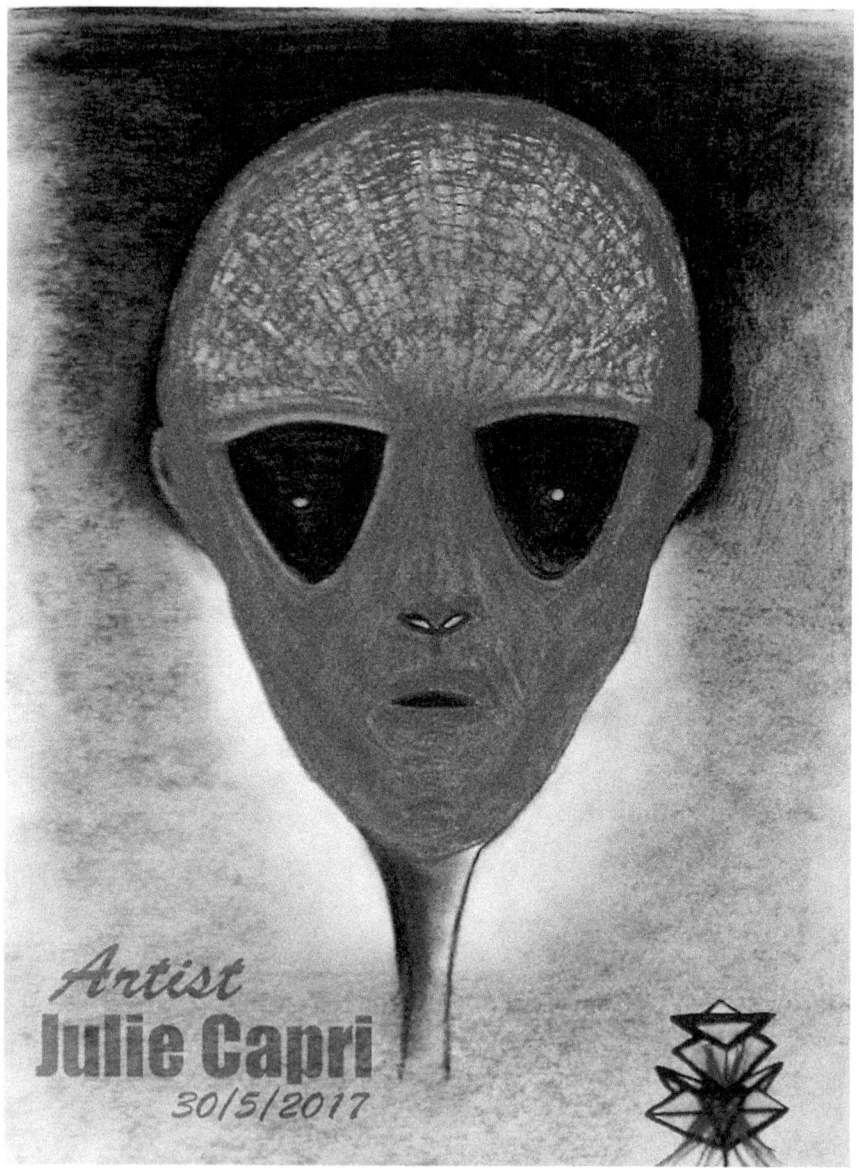

Awakening: It's time to remember who you really are

12.8.2012 Drawing #27

Artist
Julie Capri
30/5/2017

My Galactic Family

29.8.2012

Near the end of August 2012, I awoke suddenly one night, gasping for air. I'd felt like I was sinking into my body and couldn't breathe, as if my non-physical self had just returned to my physical body. I brought back my experience from the non-physical self into the physical mind to remember. From this I learnt that our consciousness does not disappear even in sleep; it is in essence who we are. So I was able to remember in great detail my non-physical self's experience even though my physical body did not go on the journey.

This is what I remembered:

I was inside a craft with dim yellow-orange lighting like a sunset at dusk. I looked around and there was someone standing beside me to my right, which I believed was a female. Someone else was sitting down just to the right in front of us, who I felt was male. They both appeared to be humanoid, wearing a one-piece suit. I instinctively knew this was a control station and thought how strange it was that it had no knobs or handles or buttons. There was just an array of lights and he was simply waving his hands across them.

To my left was an archway that led around in a circular direction, disappearing out of my sight. I remember asking them, 'Who are you and where am I?' As soon as I asked the question the answer registered within me. It was like remembering something I had forgotten, as if the answers were in my mind at the same time.

These two beings seemed familiar. I felt I had known them my whole life. The part of me that I always felt I missed as a little girl – the longing to go home even though I had a home – the part of me that always felt different – I now understood! This was my galactic family; the beings I always knew existed but could never see until now.

This experience had a massive impact on me. I spent two days crying from my longing to be with my galactic family again. I wanted to feel that unforgettable love again. I had forged a telepathic connection with them. I also felt angry that I had come back down to Earth and they had left me – as crazy as this may sound. Where I'd been had felt amazing! I had felt no worries. But coming back I felt the heaviness of Earth. The trials and tribulations that humans go through were weighing down on me.

I asked them mentally, 'Why did you leave me?'

They replied to me mentally, 'You have a mission to accomplish here on earth and you had a choice.'

> *'Why did you leave me?'*

I cried as I spoke to them. Then I also remembered my children whom I loved very much. My love for them was just as great as my longing to be with my new-found family (or were they my lost family?). I knew that Earth was where I had to be. My children were one of my main reasons for being here on Earth.

My experience of awakening to the knowledge of my galactic family was both wonderful and sad. I finally knew that I do not come from here and I have always wanted to go back 'home'. Home for me was a spaceship.

I also understood why I was seeing all these spaceships. It was a big part of my awakening, introducing me back to my roots, where I came from. I now understood that there is more to Earth. We are not the only ones, and we are connected to other beings and planets.

During the coming years, I would have more multi-dimensional experiences and my consciousness would expand even further. I studied new concepts and I began searching the internet for people who had experiences like mine. What I found was wonderful people from all around the world with an interest in UFOs, and channelers for ETs. I came across new and exciting pieces of information and concepts I had not heard of before, like alternative realities, and time and space being all one. There was so much learning to be done. I was on a mission.

1.9.2012

Early one morning, I woke up suddenly and recalled a vivid picture that was shown to me during my sleep. This was starting to be the new norm for me. I realised by now that night-time was my special time to communicate with them. I suppose it made sense as I worked all day and at night I could focus on my development.

They were showing me that my connections to the galactic people has always been there. I was shown myself at around 18 years old, standing outside in our driveway, looking up to the sky and seeing a huge mothership. I knew it was a mothership because of its shape and it had many levels. There were rows of lights right around the ship. It must have been more than ten stories high. Apparently, I'd had this experience back then in spirit and they were reminding me.

What else had I forgotten? How much of my childhood psychic experiences had related to these beings? Throughout my childhood I always had a fascination with the sky. Perhaps I knew on a subconscious level that they were there all along. And now I could see them.

Soon I drew a particularly unusual drawing. It was of a light language. It would take many years for me to find out that there were people all around the world who wrote light language, and yes it looked like mine. That tells me that we all have the ability to tap into universal knowledge if we are willing to trust and look and receive. And that information is not only given to just one person but many.

1.10.2012 Drawing #28 Light Language

10.11.2012

I never knew when my next encounter with my multi-dimensional beings was going to take place. It was always a surprise. So once again while lying awake in bed another sacred geometry appeared one night holographically, in mid-air above me. It was the same blue colour as the first visitation only this time the shape was a rectangle formation. All the time it was moving into different shapes yet still retaining its rectangle structure. It would go into patterns within itself. I could not believe my eyes. What did this sacred geometry mean? Why was it appearing to me at this stage? I truly did not understand the meaning.

No one gets taught about these kinds of experiences at school. I was questioning how many other people have these experiences. I was so lucky that my dear friend June and my close group of friends did not think I was crazy. I did feel blessed that at least I could talk to someone.

Another night, as my eyes were heavy and I was dozing off to sleep, once again I had an overwhelming urge to open them. There above me was an eight-pointed star shining like a diamond. Its presence was magnificent, and I felt the energy strong and bright, glowing as if it was showing me the way. It was by no means small. Looking from my angle I would estimate it at one metre high by one metre wide.

On the one hand I wondered why these amazing experiences were happening to me, and on the other I could not get enough of them. It was like finding treasure, but really the treasure was finding me. It had been hidden from view but now I could see. I started to see the Universe in a different way. My existence was more than meets the eye. I was starting to experience the many dimensions that I was a part of. Not just flesh and bones.

31.12.2012

It was just over a year now and the sacred geometry was still appearing to me. This time it was gold in colour, forming a beautiful flower of life. Opening and changing right before my eyes were balls of white light moving around the central structure. Faces were appearing on the sides and top but fading in and out. My heart pounded, not from fear but from feeling the sheer beautiful energy. This was not just viewing something and being separate from it: I was connected to it.

I was connected to it.

22.1.2013 Drawing #29 Essassani Energy

10.3.2013

I was in for a treat this night in March 2013. It would be the third time that the magnificent blue triangles would appear to me. I was lying in my bed as per usual. The area between my eyes, what I would call my third eye, was pulsating like never before. As the sacred geometry became clearer my whole body was moving, as if someone had a hold of my legs and was shaking me very quickly from side to side. I had no control. My whole body was pulsating.

I was also feeling the energy of this structure. This had never happened before.

The whole experience was on a whole new level and lasted for about 30 seconds. During the experience, I felt like I was out of my body or being lifted off my bed in some way. I understand now that everything holds a frequency and vibration, and what I was experiencing was the frequency of this structure. When the structure disappeared my body stopped reacting.

2014

Just when I thought I had seen it all, I was in for an incredible experience sometime in 2014. I cannot recall the exact date, but for about one week, every time I sat at the computer a wormhole about the size of a hand appeared to my right. It was fuzzing and wobbling. I really thought nothing of it at the time until I woke up one morning seeing the same structure, only a lot bigger, at the end of my bed. I would say it was about one metre high by one metre wide. I could not believe my eyes – yet there it was.

My immediate thoughts were, *Did I just come through that? Where on earth am I going at night?* I was wide awake. *OMG!* This was what I had been seeing all week but just tiny fragments of it. It only was there for a short time but long enough for me to catch sight of it. Then it was gone.

I understand now that when we open up to different dimensions, everything is layered. What you might see in this physical earth plane may not be seen from another dimension until you are that vibration. Then you will be able to perceive it as everything has its own unique frequency. You cannot perceive something until you choose to be of that vibration first. I must say, seeing a wormhole or portal at the end of your bed was amazing.

22.2.2015

My nights were certainly filled with adventures, yet I was never frightened. Curious yes, but everything I was experiencing felt normal in some strange way. One night I was shown the blue rectangular structure once more. This time it had lines and shapes creating patterns all over it. This was new to me. It was accompanied with white balls of lights moving all around the room.

This blue colour was the same colour that I had seen many years earlier in Bargo. Back then my experience was a little different. I had walked out of the bathroom into a sea of blue cloud. It was the same colour I now was experiencing with this sacred geometry. I can only describe it as walking through a thick cloud of blue but not being able to see through it. It stayed there for about one minute until it disappeared.

Not all my experiences were while I was awake. I have had many astral experiences as well. I could recall the next morning small portions of my experiences that took place in my astral body while asleep. I was taken to different places and met different people. One time I was with about 50 other humans and we were all shown two aircraft. The first one was a perfect cube shape with lines of colour running all over the outside of the craft, which was airborne. It was glowing with fluorescent colours. It would have been hovering at about 50 metres above us. The second craft was circular with lights all around the bottom. I could only see the bottom of this craft. Both would have been about 30 metres wide and could move at incredible speeds. It was fascinating to see these magnificent craft move and hover in mid-air.

Since I was present with other humans, I know that many people from around the world have been shown things too. I am not the only one. Whether they can recall their own experiences too, I don't know. All I know is my experiences are very vivid and not to be confused with dreaming while asleep.

5

Will

I was so excited about all of my amazing spiritual experiences, and I had a few close friends I could share with. Yet I started to long for that 'special somebody' in my life. Someone I could share this crazy life of mine with. Whoever it was going to be, he could certainly have to be pretty special to accept me for who I was.

I was in my mid-forties and knew meeting someone was going to be different from my twenties. I heard about a free dating site. With little money to my name, anything that was free was good in my books. So I signed up.

I was on this site for a little while and was tempted to remove my listing. But something deep inside made me stay. Some weeks went by and one gentleman eventually caught my eye. I must admit I was excited when he responded.

Up until then my life was full of amazing coincidences and the Universe was going to blow my mind even further. After a few dates with this guy, I started to notice some distinctive synchronicities. Firstly, the dating site was called Plenty of Fish. My father used to be a professional fisherman, who just happened to name his fishing trailer *Romeo*. And wouldn't you know it? This guy owned a cat called Romeo.

We found we both have the same star sign, Gemini.

The number of his house was the day of my birthday, and the number of my house was the day of his birthday.

Also my mother's favourite saying to me was always 'Where there is a will there is a way'. And yes, his name was Will – William!

It did not stop there. William had spent some 20 years working with Native American Indian pictures. Many years prior, when I was 38, I just happened to have drawn a Native American man. Upon visiting Will's house, the same Indian I had drawn was stitched into a massive rug in his office.

Our lives seemed to have mirrored each other. We had gone through so many similar hardships and life lessons, it was simply crazy. This relationship was going to be more than I had bargained for. People are always brought into our path for some learning experience whether it be for ourselves or for the other involved. Well, it was to be a learning experience for both for us. We both had certain qualities and aspects that needed changing or tweaking. We helped each other balance out the energies. I softened his hard ways and he made me stronger.

When I met Will his heart was extremely heavy as he had wanted to commit suicide six months prior. His dog saved him only to die one week later on Valentine's Day. And yes, the 14th June 2015 just happened to be the day we met each other. There is not a day that goes by where we do not finish each other's sentences or know how each other is feeling. We laugh till we cry, and we tend to take things to extremes. Yet we manage to find equilibrium in the end.

Will coming into my life was wonderful, and soon he would support me through another loss.

A passing and forgiveness

One day in 2016, my phone rang. It was my brother-in-law Tony. Tony was a matter-of-fact kind of guy. He knew there was no easy way to tell me this piece of news, so he just said it straight out: 'Your father has died.'

I was stunned. I wasn't prepared for this. I had been speaking to my dad only days before and he was in fine spirits! He was 86 and still living at home on some acreage. He had always been a strong man and was still looking after his fruit and vegetables on his property.

My father's passing was a double-edged sword for me as I had some unfinished business to take care of. For months, my heart was heavy, not from his passing but from all the anger and hurt I had been carrying for so many years. I had not been able to resolve our issues while he was living, so I was now in a situation where I alone had to deal with my feelings all by myself. It was time to heal and forgive. The releasing of emotions and forgiveness was to take nearly a year.

I suppose I was like an antenna for the Spirit World, for Dad found a way of communicating with me from the astral world. This certainly helped with my healing. He would communicate with me through the number 381 and the combination of these numbers. The house I had grown up in was number 381. One of the receipts for my father's funeral arrangements was 138, and the number property that my dad's dog had to be rehomed at was 138. Many more signs were shown to me over the coming months. In fact, for years…. For three days prior and right up to Father's Day each year, the electronics at my work would crash. Credit card machines and my computer would break down only on the dockets that were 381, 138 or 831 and so on. It was quite amazing and emotional. Sometimes I honestly believe he was just having fun and messing with my head. He had a wonderful sense of humour.

Anyway, I eventually made peace with my dad and myself, and in a crazy twist I was able to re-establish a new relationship with him in my heart. One that would make us closer than ever before. I took my power back and saw things from a different light. By releasing my pain, his pain was released also.

> *By releasing my pain, his pain was released also.*

My father continually reminds me that he is around, but now it feels different. He is always sending wonderful surprises to me and it feels nice to know he is there.

Forgiving can be a very liberating experience. It releases you and anyone else involved. I did a full circle back to unconditional love. My father gave me the opportunity to experience what true forgiveness was all about. Perhaps the shift within me at the time meant I was ready for some new experiences.

Homeless but not lost

My relationship with Will was put to the test, with us separating a few times over the next few years. When I was separated from Will for the second time, I found myself homeless for a few weeks. I never in a million years thought I would end up in this situation. However, living through hardships can give you the most amazing opportunities to really find out what you are made of. This was going to be a character-building time in my life.

To someone on the outside, my life would have appeared normal and that everything was alright. No one would have thought that I was living out of my car! The first night I said to myself, *I can do this.* I was trying to convince myself that I was alright. I figured I had a roof over my head (a car roof!), a car to get around in and a job.

Well, I wanted to get back to nature, I thought. *This is pretty close.*

So on my first night I tried to keep my life as normal as possible. I knew I wanted a strong mind and body, so I still went to the gym for my exercise after work. And then it hit me! *I'm homeless!* I had no home of my own to go back to.

So I fought the feeling and tried to feel a sense of 'home' by buying a roast for dinner. I tried to convince myself that the world was my home, and I wasn't homeless. Then another reality check – *Where am I to park my car to sleep?* I thought this was going to be easy. Well, that was an understatement.

73

Knowing my children were safe with their father was a comfort at least.

I proceeded to three different places before I found myself right back at the carpark where I work. I thought my back seat was going to be comfortable. Nope! It seemed like hours before I could get comfortable. I experimented with every possible angle and resorted to lying the front seat down and finding a reasonable position. *Well, this is progress. Alleluia.* I am sure the angels would have had a chuckle to themselves.

Being summer on the Gold Coast, it was a mighty hot night to have the windows up. But I needed to for safety. I survived the first night. I wasn't scared but I was on alert and very aware of my surroundings.

The next morning I was wondering what to do for breakfast. Then I remembered a voucher I had been given two months previously for an all-you-can-eat breakfast at Mantra Hotel. Thank goodness I had hung onto it! What a great time to use it.

I felt such immense gratitude that I promised myself that I was going to do an act of kindness every day despite my current circumstances. And that's what I did. On my first day, I gave a stranger some credit in a photocopying machine that I had been using. The second day, I gave some potatoes I had bought to a lady in a car park prior to my doctor's appointment.

I just had to trust the Universe was going to be on my side.

I was still to some degree carrying a fair amount of self-judgement. I was so worried about the appearance of my car, so I tried to keep it tidy. I didn't want anyone to know I was living out of my car. I suppose it was just taking pride. But I instinctively didn't fall into victimhood and had to trust in the invisible force that had guided me in my life. I had to give my situation to Creation and let go of control thinking.

I decided to make the most of the situation and worked an extra shift to get more money. Besides, I was already at work and where else could I go? One night I saw a homeless man sitting outside my work and I thought how lucky I was. I had better living conditions than him. At least I had a car with a roof over my head.

I continued to do my good deeds for the day even if it was simply talking to a total stranger and listening to them. I knew the world is full of heartaches of some description. Doing good things kept my spirits up. It was surprising how accustomed I had become to my circumstances. It did not take me long to get used to what I had to do. Even though I had no bed to sleep in, it did not matter. I was not going to concentrate on the six to seven hours of my day sleeping in my car. There was 24 hours in a day, and I chose to focus on the rest of the hours that made up my day.

I was not going to let others' points of view determine or define who and what I was. Faith was challenging me on one level. *How much do I truly have and am I believing in it?* I felt I was being asked to trust that I was living exactly where I was meant to be. I pondered that we humans sometimes choose our experiences without real conscious awareness of what we are creating, but they are always for the soul's highest experience. I do believe that I was led to these pondering and internal conclusions. It was all part of the lesson I was going through.

Sometimes we have to walk different paths to really experience others' points of view. We can only imagine situations. But this was real. I was homeless and it was happening right now. I felt myself being told:

'There is nothing in your life that is wrong. You turned up in a physical body to partake in another day on earth. Simple.'

After a week of living in my car, it became clear to me that this had become my home, my sanctuary, a place where I felt safe. I was starting to live in a non-judgemental state. It did not matter where I rested. It could be camping in a forest, by a lake, by a river, in a house, apartment or even on a street. It did not matter as it was my relationship with where I was that mattered. Nothing else.

Living through hardships shapes our character, allowing us to remember how strong we are within. There is a sense of freedom that comes from not having a home. It was something I did not realise. I became one with nature once again. And I had another profound thought one day: *Living in a house restricts you by giving you walls to exist in, boxing you in, giving you a false sense of security.*

From what? I asked. My thoughts ran rapidly. *To keep bad people away, to accumulate things, to hang on to things. And never do we take them with us when we leave Earth. To give the appearance of wealth, the appearance of success, the appearance of superiority.*

I now realised why people purchase motorhomes; it gave them such a sense of freedom. I decided to be a willing participant in allowing my higher self to guide me. I instinctively knew it would lead me to where I needed to be – at exactly the right time for whatever my higher purpose was. Instead of focusing of needing a home, I started to let go and be grateful for my home that was going to show up.

I knew I had to be proactive in creating my home. I allowed the power of the Creative Force to guide me to reach my dream. Meanwhile, I kept doing something for someone else, sometimes after the Universe nudged me in unusual directions. Like telling me to go and buy a fruit juice at a new shop that had just opened. It just so happened I had received some tips that day and was feeling pretty good. It seemed to be a good idea. While I was there a young girl asked me where I worked. And it just so happened that she had always wanted to work there as well. I told her to mention my name, and maybe this helped her as she did get a job there. The Creative Force was working on my dream, but I was helping others with theirs.

I ended up finding a lovely real estate lady who really listened to my situation. I could feel my new home was at arm's length and I was filled with feelings of gratitude even before she found me a place. Which she did! It was a quaint little beach shack minus the beach! It had been renovated inside, but the outside was rather old looking. It did not matter; this was going to be my home. I found everything in a second-hand shop that I needed to start my new place. And it was all practically new.

On my last night of being homeless, I felt I had come to a different state of being. I had reflected on my life and observed the world through new eyes. I had evolved. Been awakened. Some of the key lessons I took from this experience were:

- Your darkest hour becomes your greatest achievement.
- It is up to you to give each day meaning. What are you going to give not take?
- You sometimes don't see the full picture till the end; until all the pieces of the puzzle are put together to show you the bigger picture.

Here is the final reflection I diarised on my last night of homelessness:

My experiences have made me humbler and more compassionate than I already was.

I no longer want to think in a judgemental frame of mind about myself or anybody else.

I have made peace with myself and take responsibility for everything in my life.

I am co-creating all my experiences.

My situation was not anyone's fault. I was only experiencing a set of decisions and circumstances, one after another.

To have more faith than ever before that Creation looks after you...

Follow and trust your gut feelings and go with the flow as it will lead to the right place at the right time.

You don't have to make life a struggle. It only becomes a struggle when you resist and insist on how things are meant to be.

*I am not going to let my circumstances dictate who I am.
I have more of an appreciation of life and how I have
been living and what changes I am going to implement.
Relax a little more and be more kind to myself...
Be able to stop and be more in the moment...
Take in your surroundings more.
Embrace what comes to you no matter the
appearances and only choose a positive outcome from
anything that happens. Circumstances do not matter,
only states of being.*

I had kept my homelessness a secret from everyone, even Will. Call it being stubborn, call it independence or pride. Probably a combination of all three. I suppose my upbringing gave me a sense of toughness that only experience can give you.

Eventually, Will and I got back together after this, and there were a few more ups and downs and small separations, until we had complete trust and belief in each other. When all that was left was love, we both could feel secure that we were not going to get hurt any more.

Being guided by your heart feels completely different to been guided by your mind.

Synchronicities

Will and I both experienced certain numbers repeatedly showing up in our lives. Carl Jung calls this 'synchronicity'. Synchronicities are meaningful coincidences that have no causal relationships but are meaningfully related. I've already shared how my father's presence was often communicated with a combination of the numbers 381.

The 1111 numbers have also been with me for the last 11 years and Will has experienced this phenomenon for the last five years. For me it all started on the 19/01/2009, which is broken down numerologically to 1/1/11. I was staying at a hotel on the Gold

Coast on the 11th floor in Room 1111. This got my attention, and since then 1111 has continued to do so.

I see this prompt on signs, cars and clocks. The 1111 time prompt is a universal concept. The collective unconscious of the humans that occupy Earth has

> *The 1111 time prompt is a universal concept.*

created this time prompt for the awakening of humanity. You could say that whenever it is seen, it gives us a moment to remember who we are and what connection we have with the Creator.

Whenever Will and I see the 1111 time prompt, we say to each other 'I love you'. We started this from the beginning of our relationship.

Sometimes synchronicities occurred around meeting people randomly who were to play a role, either significant or insignificant, in my life. One was meeting Gay, my first spiritual mentor. Another instance occurred around finding the right surgeon to aid in healing of my foot.

In 2019, the injury from my foot when I was 17 was taking its toll, and I believed it was related to the pain I'd had inside for so long regarding my father. It was time for change. The feet represent the ability to move forward. I knew I had changed, so I believed I was ready to heal my physical body now as well. I had been struggling for a long time, not being able to walk properly, and I had to match my body with the new person I had become.

I had spent the previous two years processing all the emotional hurt relating to my foot and now I was ready for the new me. Will, being the caring soul that he is, was massaging my painful foot one night as he always did for me, when out of the blue he said, 'We are finding a doctor to do the surgery on your foot'.

This is where the synchronicity in my life just shines. The first surgeon I went to see unfortunately said the operation was too complicated for him and he referred me to another orthopaedic surgeon, Dr Won. It was not exactly the news I wanted to hear, but nevertheless he pointed me in the right direction.

That weekend I did my shift at work and came across a lady with a walking stick who needed to elevate her foot as she had just had a foot reconstruction operation four months earlier. And would you know it? Dr Won did her surgery. The Universe has my attention when things are shown to me double and triple times. It's saying, 'Go for it!'

I proceeded to make an appointment only to find that there was a 10-month waiting list. So I decided to put my name down on a cancellation list. Well, it would have only been two months later that I dreamed of the receptionist calling me to say they had a cancellation and asking if I could come in. The next day at 9 am, the phone rang, and it was the receptionist telling me of an opening for an appointment. Talk about communication from the Spirit World giving me a right royal message loud and clear!

My surgery took place nine months later. It would take 12 months to make a full recovery. I spent 16 days in hospital, three months in a moon boot, three months learning to walk again, and another six months to regain full strength of my foot and redness and swelling to subside.

I am now the proud owner of a 4-inch plate, 14 screws, and a couple of pins and clamps. I have a new strong foot to carry me for the rest of my life. I figure that those few extra spare parts in my body make me a little bionic and strong, just like the strong person I always was.

Synchronicity was at work again when Will and I decided on a complete lifestyle and business sea change. Will had already experienced success in business long before I met him, and now he was supporting my dream to become a successful businesswoman. It was special now that we could develop a business together. We opened a company called BookToday. The fruits of our labour are still to flourish and in time we will have a successful online booking travel company.

I continued to trust that the Universe has always got my back. It's when we are going with the flow that things just happen. We have to trust that the Universe has always got the path laid out for us. We may not know what the path is, but do not let the unknowing make you fear. Instead I have learnt to ask, 'What surprises do you have for me?'

We were soon in for a wonderful surprise!

Our rental lease was up; the owners were not going to renew the lease and we had to vacate in February 2020, just before COVID-19 hit Australia. Will and I had decided that it was time to get ready to promote our business. We were to go around Australia in a motorhome promoting BookToday. To do that we had to make some changes. We sold all our furniture – and I mean everything except for three small pieces of sentimental furniture. We packed up our personal belongings and put them in storage. All we had left in the house was what going to be in the motorhome. The motorhome we didn't yet have! We were running on faith.

I had been on the search for a motorhome through all the major companies, hoping that someone was going to sponsor us but to no avail. Time was ticking away. While having a sentimental moment I contacted a beautiful couple I had met one year earlier at work. I wanted to know how they were going, not even thinking about our motorhome predicament. I was so happy to hear their voices. In the next breath Jill said, 'Everything is good, but Kel is having trouble selling his motorhome.' I do believe my heart skipped a beat! As soon as I saw Will I told him. We were both so excited!

Within the next 24 hours we were at their doorstep, ready and willing to be owners of a motorhome.

I have learnt that you must be open and trusting in the timing of the Universe. I never gave up on our dream. No matter how many times I heard, 'No I can't help you,' I never gave up. I stayed open to all the ways that the Universe provides, and sometimes help comes quite contrary to your expectations. For example, the time Will and I had visitors right above us in the sky!

So why the ETs?

A few years ago, I was asked to speak at a conference on the Gold Coast called 'Transformational Shift', the subject being UFOs amongst other things. My wonderful Will put together my PowerPoint presentation. I could not wait for this opportunity to speak.

One week before the conference, Will and I were driving through Tugun on the Gold Coast when I looked out of the front windscreen and noticed a metallic light in the sky. 'What is that up in the sky?' I asked Will.

We pulled over and Will got his camera and started filming. It was straight in front of us. We had a clear view as it was a clear blue sky. We kept rewinding the footage, seeing all the details in close-up. The colours were amazing! I believe whoever was in that craft wanted me to see them for I was able to share the footage with the audience the following week at the conference. I also have the footage on my website. www.juliecapri.com

I know for real that the phrase 'we are not alone' is correct. If you think we are the only civilization in the entire galaxy, you may be in for a few surprises. In our galaxy alone there are thousands of different species of races, some humanoid and some not. Here is an amusing concept for you to think about: Humans have defined anyone living outside of our planet as ETs or aliens. What if we were to turn this around and look at it from an ET perspective. What would they think of us? Would we be called 'alien' from their perspective? Can you see how humans at times are limited in their thinking and it's time to expand our thinking?

To begin with, we are not alien to other ETs at all as our DNA is linked to some other species existing in our Universe. We could say that these beings are our

> *We are affiliated to other planetary life that exists in our Universe.*

galactic family. We are entering a new era of connection with other races and we are remembering our connection as part of Earth's evolution. The feelings of separation and disassociation will no longer be thought of, but instead be replaced with the knowledge that we are affiliated to other planetary life existing in our Universe. This will be the next norm for planet Earth. There will come a day when humanity will look back and think, 'How could we have not known about each other?' and 'Why did it take so long for information like this to be disclosed to the public?'

Planet Earth has had contact with beings from outer space for thousands of years. Our pyramids in Egypt are just one location where we can clearly see this interaction. The carvings and manuscripts clearly show us that the gods depicted in their carvings were the ETs. The construction of these magnificent structures is in precise alignment with the Orion constellation of stars, and the geographical coordinates are the same numerical number of the speed of light. The dimensions of the pyramids are exactly the polar radius of the Earth. There was so much technology that was given to the people of that time regarding free energy, maths and astrology. The famous Nicola Tesla was fascinated with the pyramids of Egypt, and through his years of research, he mathematically concluded that the numbers 3,6 and 9 were keys to the Universe within the sacred geometry of these magnificent structures.

Contact has never stopped reaching our planet. Even in the last 100 years I can make mention of a couple of well-known 'contactees' such as Steven M Greer and Michel Desmarquet. There are plenty more for you to investigate on the internet. For example, Laura Eisenhower, the great-granddaughter of the late Dwight Eisenhower, shares incredible knowledge and evidence of the interactions that have taken place between our planet Earth and beings from other parts of the Universe. There is so much information on her website and in YouTube videos where she shares her evidence and knowledge.

She is just one of the many awakened souls around the planet who are sharing knowledge. One of the first well-known contactees in our 20th Century was Billy Meier. The Pleiadeans first made contact with Meier when he was five years old. His collections of photos, film footage and much written knowledge has helped us understand more about our Universe.

I could not go on without mentioning the famous Area 51 in the Nevada Desert in the USA. There have been so many cover ups about this place! Finally, people who were associated with Area 51 and others from around the world are making disclosures, leading to more material on the internet and social media. There are so many eyewitness accounts from all over the world of UFOs in the skies today, with numerous photos and videos, that it is now impossible to deny the existence of these crafts. Our planet Earth is involved in something much bigger than scientists and astrologists care to share. There is an old saying, 'Look and you shall find'. It is up to you now to look and find for yourself.

We now live in a modern age of technology and information is more readily available than ever before. I urge you to trust in your own guidance and learn to feel what is right for you. Do your own research. There are many people all over the planet who have had connections with beings in many ways. To say that one way or one piece of information is better than another would be to deny each its own truth or expression. Because each of us has our own unique experience, we all can access and receive information differently. But altogether it is part of a much bigger picture.

We have been kept in the dark and it is time for the correct knowledge and information to be shared to the people of the world. Beautiful benevolent beings are waiting to be recognised and acknowledged in the same light and love that they truly represent.

> *Beautiful benevolent beings are waiting to be recognised and acknowledged...*

The movie makers in Hollywood have for quite some time been portraying an unrealistic negative image of ETs, depicting most as vengeful and attacking humans on Earth. They are unconsciously brainwashing humans into a state of fear. So there is no way that beings from other planets are going to have mass landing of spaceships on our planet Earth until we the humans come to accept their existence and that they are not going to kill or harm us.

Not all ETs are in a negative category; there are many positive, loving races. There are races that do not experience the duality that humans have created and experience here on Earth. This is because their spiritual evolution has grown beyond duality. This type of level would be categorized as a 6D dimension as there is no incarnation into a physical body. Earth is currently categorized as a 3D dimensional reality. The ascension process that Earth is currently experiencing is all about humanity experiencing a 3D reality and integrating and experiencing 4D and 5D realities whilst still on Earth. It's about living on a 3D plane with heightened spiritual awareness, experiencing a new type of Earth. *The Awakening Teachings* in Part 2 of this book will give you some guidance. As you grow in spiritual consciousness and awareness so too will your experiences.

I cannot blame Hollywood alone. It is also a lack of knowledge. Schools do not have the appropriate curriculum set up for higher learning. We need to introduce topics such as spiritual awakening, psychic development, learning to self-heal the body with sound and light, and galactic history instead of ancient history. The current teachers do not possess the knowledge or skills. If they did, they would not be allowed to express these topics and would be ridiculed. One day we will look back and wonder how we did not teach these topics at school.

Governments from all around the world have yet to disclose to the public all the knowledge they have on UFOs. The media is so controlled by the Dark State or Cabal that they are told what to broadcast, and most of the time it is fear-based news to keep you in a state of fear.

Several years ago, I had the privilege to have a conversation with a lady who disclosed her nightly experiences with the ETs (Greys) visiting her. It was an incredible conversation and yet it saddened me that she withheld so much information from everyone around her as she was afraid of what people would think. It is time for more conversations like these to take place in an atmosphere where messengers are not discriminated against or misunderstood.

There are some who do speak out. For example, a beautiful lady by the name of Gosia has had direct contact with the Taygeta people who are from the Pleiades star system. You can access a lot of information from her YouTube channel, Cosmic Agency. Not only will you find how the different ET space craft operate and their technological advances, but so much information on a variety of topics including other races, gravity and space travel.

This whole topic alone would require a whole book. There is a lot of information for you to research on the internet, Nonetheless, I thought you would like to know of a few races that have come to my attention:

- The Yahyel – responsible for the UFO sightings of March 1997, commonly known as the Phoenix Lights. Thousands witnessed the events across the State of Arizona, North America.
- Nordic/Pleiadeans – humanoids with blonde hair, blue eyes and a height of 6 to 7 feet
- Sassani – a hybrid that has developed and is genetically linked to humans
- The Greys – the more predominant extra-terrestrial beings that we have heard of, especially from the 1960s
- Reptilians – tall and scaly
- Anunnaki – one of the earliest to visit our planet
- Andromedans – far more advanced than we are with an average lifespan of 2000 years
- Arcturians – main race is about 5 feet tall with large almond eyes. Highly creative in arts, music and engineering. They are also responsible for most of the crop circles we see on Earth.

I have only mentioned a few. There are many more versions and variations of these within each race.

6

My Journey Continues

Throughout all my real-life experiences I have continued to experience my sacred geometry visiting me. Each visit is always special. Over the years I have come to understand more and more about what I have been shown, especially to do with numbers and shapes and how they are connected.

While not everyone has such spiritual and otherworld experiences as these, you will know by now that I've experienced the highs and lows, love and sorrows of life just like everybody else. Perhaps like you. My human family had some real challenges. I was not born into a life of prestige but of challenge and contradiction. Of good and bad. But through my sharing I hope that you are reassured that no matter your life circumstances, you can overcome adversity and survive. We can shift from victim to survivor, and forgiveness is very much possible. It is a powerful experience.

Hindsight is a wonderful thing. To look back and see what has happened in your life, learn from it and redefine what you wish to experience for your future is a wonderful opportunity. Would I change anything that has happened in my life? No. All my life experiences have shaped me to be who I am today. Even in writing this book I have experienced great pleasure, joy and healing. I am filled with gratitude.

As you can now see, my experiences with the ETs and my life of psychic experiences fuelled a drive in me to seek esoteric knowledge, which continues today. My learnings over many years of study and experiences are brought together now as *The Awakening Teachings*, in Part 2. All that I have been through, and learned, is for the purpose of reminding you – all of humanity – who we are, to assist humanity's awakening. You will learn about Source and Creation, Fear versus Love, the Power of Manifestation, Death and Consciousness, and Time and Space.

Throughout the following information I use the words 'Source', 'Creation' and 'All That Is' – even 'God'. To me they mean the same thing – the ultimate supreme energy force which is in everything and is key to our incredible power, which we have forgotten. My purpose for sharing the key concepts within *Awakening Teachings* is to help you awaken

> *It is now your moment to remember who you really are and who humanity is.*

much knowledge that you already hold within you. It is now your moment to remember who you really are and who humanity is.

The year of finishing the final draft of this book was 2020, which is so ironic as it reminds me of 20/20 vision. This is an opportunity to look back on the past or look forward to the future from 2021 and finetune our perspective, or vision.

In saying this, this concept of time, with a past and future, is only a man-made psychological experience. Time is a construct of single moments repeated one after another and experienced from a different point of view each time. I will expand on this topic of time further on where I will else reflect on living in this 3D world on Earth from a spiritual perspective through applying the Awakening Teachings into your life.

It is about *your* awakening. My hope is that you can start living life from a higher perspective as your awakening unfolds. My awakening has given me a new sense of reality. May it do the same for you as you discover who you really are. More and more people are awakening and are being shown their own connections to the ETs through sightings and experiences like my own, and their oneness with Source.

Awakening comes when you are searching and when you are ready for your awakening. Are you ready?

PART 2

THE AWAKENING TEACHINGS

7

Source and Creation

Mankind has come up with the notion of praying to something or someone. Throughout the Ages humans on Earth have projected many versions of God, based on their limited knowledge and understanding at that time, using deities and religions. We have reflected our version of God's qualities as we perceive them at any given era of time. The God concept has been represented in a myriad of ways from a vengeful cruel God to a powerful God. These human concepts demonstrate our belief. This understanding (or lack of) is due to the concept that we are separate from Source. This has led to mankind seeing itself as somehow beneath or lower than their God.

I have news for you: God is Creator, not of just one Universe but of infinite probable existences – of everything that one could imagine and more. There is no space that Creation has not filled including us. We are not separate. We are made of Creation; therefore, it is in us not outside of us.

Before you took on human form, your soul consciousness knew only oneness. There was no separation from Source. You have been created perfectly with nothing lacking. Creation's innate structure is to create, and this has been embedded within you. Just as Creation expresses itself with free will and can create, expressing and experiencing all that is to experience, Creation/Source gave humanity – you – the same ability.

Existence is in a constant state of manifesting and choosing from the infinite choices available. When you believe that there is some sort of lack within yourself, this perception has been created by your ego mind and needs to be corrected. The perception that you can change what Creation has created is erroneous, as is the notion that what is perfect to begin with is imperfect or lacking in some way.

When we decided to take on human form, we formed a belief that we were separated from Creation itself. However, we are the sons of Creation, figuratively speaking, and we are Creation creating. We have not separated from Source; we are Source. We are the very thing that we think we are not. That is why we have configured the concept of 'God' – something bigger than ourselves. But in essence we are all gods.

> *We have not separated from Source; we are Source.*

When humanity is ready to awaken from this error in judgement (the erroneous notion of separation) and right thinking is in place, the world will come to see everyone equally as brothers and sisters and creators. Truth will then come into your existence. This correction in judgement brings peace, which can only be found inside you.

If you can refocus your attention to your inner Self, the truth will unveil itself to you.

All is one and one is all

Everything that you experience is felt individually, as an aspect of Creation, yet each experience is part of what makes the whole reality. Creation is just one atom and when Creation decided to expand that one atom into a multitude of smaller ones, Creation itself is each atom, which continues to still be a part of what makes up the whole. Everything is connected to everything else. *The all is one and the one is all.*

Imagine you are looking into a kaleidoscope and seeing the many different combinations of colours and shapes moving and intertwining with one another. Now picture everything physical around you as a movement of energy and colours, with the ability to move through one another and blend with no boundaries. There are an infinite number of possibilities that can exist all at the same time.

Now, extending this concept to the Earth you live on, picture the beautiful ocean on this Earth and each of us as a drop of that ocean. Each tiny separate droplet is the ocean. And when put back together these droplets make the whole ocean.

Extend this concept to the planets, the Universes and the galaxies. You are still part of that bigger picture; you make up the picture. However, there is no end as Creation never stops creating and we are all linked in some way. We are all interlinked pieces of the bigger picture. The creator is Love, and so we are of Love. Love is the universal 'glue' that interlinks all the pieces of the bigger picture.

Knowing we are all of the same source and pure of heart, there are only two ways through which we experience life. One is from the ego's perspective (illusion) and the other is from the perspective of Source. This takes some explaining.

Ego's illusion vs the perspective of Source

We are in illusion when we think that the people around us are 'real'. In fact, we have a version of them within our world, which we have created. The *experiences* are real, and the people are just actors in your play. We are each projecting out the play we wish to experience. We then have to take responsibility for making the movie or play up in the first place. *See Chapter 10 for more info on this topic.*

So you created your life consciously before coming to Earth, but when you took incarnation, the veil of forgetfulness was drawn to the memory of these things. It is time to wake up from your slumber. If you choose to now see a different point of view, you can consider that any pain or sorrow you sometimes feel has all been created by you through the different scenarios you have been creating.

Let's look at an event that requires you to experience the act of forgiveness. Someone has hurt or offended you and you *think* that you need to forgive them. This is usually the first reaction. Remember, you have projected out from your being and you made everything up in the first place. Everything is not technically real, and there is nothing to forgive as everything is a projection from inside yourself. Let's explain it further.

It's the unconscious mind that is projecting out the movie to be experienced. The ego will try its hardest to convince you that your body is real. It does this through manipulating your mind. Your mind will recall certain memories to identify that you are you. It does this by making you take note of any pain, suffering, even annoyances and sickness you have gone through, taking your attention from the Now where reality is experienced. The ego makes you drift off to the past, making your mind go to distant thoughts. This is the ego at its best.

Your truest origins are eternal, and when you come from the Creator or Source perspective, nothing that is not real can harm you or affect you. You have conceived the idea of separation from Creator, which has led to your erroneous projections in this world. This means that everything you see is fundamentally based on the idea of separation and the notion that we have separate, individual bodies. When our perspective is flowing from Source, we realise and understand that we are one.

All masters have acquired this understanding of oneness and that there is no separation of anything. This realisation is awakening from the dream of unconsciousness. You realise that

The world is not coming at you; the world is done through you.

you are not the effect of the dream; you created the dream. The world is not coming at you; the world is done through you. You realise that you are not the effect in the dream, but the cause. It is your projection in the first place.

The Creator wants you to know that there is nothing to fear, and that you are not the body you think you are. You are the same as the Creator. You never separated from the Creator to begin with; you are inexplicably connected. I go as far as to say you are Creator too. You are also one with everybody else. The third perspective (which paradoxically is the ability to achieve the first two) is the ability to forgive. This is how the ego is wiped away. When your thoughts are coming from a place of cause by you, you understand that you can forgive everyone as they have not done anything and have never left heaven. Couple this perspective with the first and second, that you are one with the Creator and one with everyone else, and now you will see the whole, true perspective!

The others you are engaging with are just characters in the play you wrote. In fact, you have both been writing separate scripts, yet you are a part of each other's play and dramas within the play. So nobody is guilty of anything really because it's all made up to seem as if it is real. *You were projecting from an illusory place to begin with.*

The physical components of what you see are basically nothing more than a single atom. And each atom is holding a different frequency and expression of who they are. We have nearly 7 billion people on our planet, with each person experiencing life with their own versions of reality and these are existing all at once. And let us not forget the other billions of forms that exist elsewhere in the Universe. Each individual is possessing their own frequencies and having their own belief systems, which are all correct.

Yes, they are all correct.

You may first be asking, 'They cannot be all correct, can they? There must be just one correct truth?' Yes, they are correct. Each person is creating their own version of reality, of whatever they think is correct for them no matter how it may look from someone else's perspective. One must change one's perspective to the concept of right and wrong and understand that it is energy and intentions that are expressed in life. The universal law is that the energy given out by you will be returned to you. Creation does not miss anything. Please understand that there are many acts that do cause much harm to others and there are consequences.

Humans tend to become judge and jury, so remember that the universe is layered, and many perspectives can be experienced from the one experience. You could say that all life begins from a neutral perspective and point of view until we decide what it means for us. *I share more on this in Chapter 9.*

From the same atom

To reiterate, the people that make up Earth, the plants, trees, animals and all the other planets and Universes in all the other galaxies are made from the same atom. We are all connected. The entire structure of existence springs from the same atom that expresses itself in billions of different ways. Because we are from the same atom, we can communicate with each other. We are the same.

If you were to change every atom that you see around you – in the chair you sit on, the tree you lean on and every human – and brought it back to the single atom before it took form, you would see we are all the same. What you are seeing with your physical eyes are particular atoms mixed to form new structures. We are all originate from a single atom which expressed and multiplied itself into many different forms, with all necessary information contained in every atom.

We are also seeing the same projected dream that is being created from the non-physical form of a human. That is because one or more people are projecting and agreeing on a thing or a focus collectively, wishing to experience it. That is why we all have common experiences.

The one mind of the Creator, in a way, has been split into many different parts so that it sees and experiences life through different points of view or perspectives. The Creator is many, and 'He' is one. He is like an ocean. If you removed the ocean water one cup at a time till there was no ocean left, all the individual cups of water make up the whole ocean.

Everything that takes form symbolises Creation. In its original state, Creation is essentially spirit, having no form or gender. Why would Creation go forth to create an image of 'himself' if he has none? Creation has free will to make any form he wishes. Likewise, we were created in this image to create whatever form we wanted.

Chapter Summary

- *Humanity at large is living under the illusion of separation from Source.*
- *Love is the universal 'glue' that interlinks all the pieces of the bigger picture.*
- *It is time to awaken.*
- *We are one with all Creation.*
- *We have free will to create any form we wish.*

8

Consciousness at Work

We humans are always fascinated by what happens after death. At death you will lose your physical body, but you do not die. It is impossible. Death is an illusion. When your physical body appears to stop and die, your higher non-physical mind keeps right on going. It never ceases. Everything physical is an illusion. Just as a coin has two sides, so does life. One reality is physical and the other spirit, yet the two sides make up the whole. You can make the transition from one side to the other so easily. Memory survives death.

Everything that you can imagine – your body, brain, body, your entire Universe – are all projections of the higher non-physical mind. It is all symbolic of just one thought.

Conscious vs unconscious

When enough specific awareness of frequency is directed to a specific point, you create your body. While in a body, you then have many opportunities to develop an awareness of who you truly are. Your consciousness expands to the understanding that you are both physical and non-physical. Your unconscious mind is totally unaware, otherwise it would be conscious. Your unconscious mind is under the domination of thoughts from your physical mind. Many of these thoughts are part of a collective momentum that are shared by everyone on the planet.

Everything that you experience in the human body is in a constant state of change. Death is simply part of the process of change. You exist; the notion that existence ceases when one leaves the body is nonsensical. It is impossible for existence to not exist.

While you had a physical body, your cells were always in a constant state of dying and becoming new. This is a dying and rebirth of oneself over and over again at a cellular level, which makes up your whole physical body. Have you ever stopped to realise that if the cells of your body did not renew themselves you would not exist?

You may change form as little or as many times as you like and the essence of you, your consciousness, will always continue to be there even after a physical life on earth. All the people on planet Earth are playing out their own infinite versions of themselves at any one moment. Each has their own frequency and carry their own set of belief systems and versions of how they experience life here on Earth.

When you pass over to the other side, you still have consciousness and know that you have had a physical body. Whatever belief systems you hold about death and what happens after that will be your experience. For example, a 'good' Christian will see Jesus Christ and think they are in heaven. A 'good' Muslim will think they are in Paradise and a 'good' Mormon will think they are in one of the predicted kingdoms of glory. If you think that no one will be there when you cross over, you may experience that notion as well for a short period of time. Or if you think that you are going to meet all the dearly departed you will experience this as well.

Here is how reality works

So how does reality work, in short? Your soul projects out the desire to have a physical existence on planet Earth. You manifest a body of your choosing to explore the thought of having a physical experience on Earth. Within this construct are many versions of

'Earth'. I am not referring to the physical Earth for there is only one. I am referring to the different versions of reality that are experienced through you. Let's call this physical Earth 'the stage'. All lifetimes that you may be choosing are happening at the same time and you are only conscious of the one you are in now. And Earth just happens to be one of your lifetimes.

Now, time to use your imagination…

In this stage or playground there is nature, other souls like yourself, physical things you have constructed, and lots of collective beliefs systems that you and other souls have all agreed upon. For example, you may say there are trees. They will provide oxygen for us to survive, and we will give them the colours green and brown. This and many other ideas form your 'playground', Earth. The physical structure stays the same no matter what version of reality you choose to experience and think through your physical being.

Now that we have the stage to play on, you also determine how long you wish to stay here as well.

So your consciousness forms matter, and your thoughts existed before you had a body (and after you have a body). Your consciousness is alive and well and will not cease just because your body has ceased. Telepathic communication from those who have passed over exists because a physical body is not required for them to communicate. We think babies are not aware. However, it is only that their bodies have not developed enough to share their thoughts and awareness through words. We humans come to Earth containing all

> *The collective consciousness of humanity has chosen to experience the denial of remembering who and where they came from.*

the necessary knowledge, and we have to go through a process for the body to grow and develop for us to express this knowledge. There are also varying degrees of knowledge and awareness.

My main point is that the world is created from your interior reality. The solid matter you see is merely atoms and molecules of projected consciousness. To fully understand the definition of consciousness, you must be able to see from the perspective of your origin or higher perspectives other than the constructs of the physical mind and body. However, there is a reason why many of us have placed ourselves under a limited experience: The collective consciousness of humanity has chosen to experience the denial of remembering who and where they came from.

This was a collective decision of those who wished to experience life in a physical form on planet Earth. For now Earth is awakening and humans are sensing a new awareness of consciousness. The physical Earth still has its form and it too is changing in sync with the collective consciousness of humanity.

The shadow work

You have both consciousness and the unconsciousness residing within yourself. It is so important that you work on the aspects of yourself that you are not conscious of. I refer to it as doing 'the shadow work' of yourself.

As you awaken fully to knowing who you truly are, you will find that you become conscious of the unconscious side of yourself. It's about being conscious in the moment when you are about to react to situations or say things from behaviours and beliefs systems that you have learnt without realising it. Becoming conscious is about taking ownership of the unconscious side of you and undoing or unlearning these unwanted beliefs and reprogramming yourself through right thought and action.

So are you conscious or unconscious of what you are manifesting in your life? Or are you just existing, wondering why certain experiences or emotions keep repeating themselves again and again?

I have often heard people saying, 'This happens to me all the time'. Or they ask, 'Why does this keep happening to me?' The question they should be asking themselves is *Why am I attracting this to me?* When you are creating, it basically comes from the consciousness and subconscious parts of yourself. The subconscious stores all the stuff you have picked up on over your life. The unconscious programming can sabotage your life if you are not aware of it. You can be acting out the programming and belief systems from other people that you have taken on, and you are then reacting blindly. How many times have you reacted to things because your subconscious reacted and not the conscious you?

How much of your life, like mine was, has been spent always trying to please someone else's expectations of you? Your mind does not contain a point of reference for comparison, so it will tell you that, no, you can't possibly think of yourself, and you feel guilty about even having the thought. You may not even realise you are feeling guilty, it is so unconscious.

When you start to live in alignment with your own truth from being aware of your inner life, you may also realise how much you have neglected yourself. As you start to get to know yourself once again, you may realise your wants, needs and dreams have been put on the back burner. You have been preoccupied with other people's views of what is best for you. When you follow someone else's view you are giving your power away.

Please don't get me wrong. Most people will always say that they were only thinking about what was best for you. What they were really telling you is what they would do from their point of view, that's all.

Perhaps it is time for you to say to everyone in your life that it is okay for you to not feel guilty about thinking about yourself, to experience whatever you wish to experience. Of course, I'm not promoting here that you do things that bring harm to others. There are consequences. We still must be of service where we can, but only if it is something that we each truly feel within us to do, following our personal expectations and not someone else's agenda. The world you live in, the reality you are forming, has largely been based on outside influences. You have been unconsciously programmed about what to think and how to feel, with the fear of God being placed into you. This is a man-made concept.

It is so important to become aware of your thoughts and ask yourself, 'Am I thinking from the now or the past?' Become conscious of your thoughts and be truly present from moment to moment. *In Chapter 10 we will look more closely at your power of manifestation in creating your desired life.*

Chapter Summary

- *Death is an illusion. Consciousness continues.*
- *It is essential to recognise unconscious programming and man-made concepts.*
- *Be conscious of what you are creating or allowing in your life.*
- *It is okay to put yourself first.*

9

Fear Versus Love

The perception of separation that we discussed in Chapter 7 brings about the notion of fear, which again has been created by us. Fear is the opposite to our highest and truest expression, which is love.

Health and wellbeing are experienced as inner peace, and illness occurs when we deviate from the inner focus and operate erroneously through the outer. When you are in fear mode, you are believing that somehow you are going to be hurt in some way. But it's all in the physical mind. A true miracle occurs when you understand that through your free will you can accept or deny being afraid. Recognise the truth that no one can hurt you unless you create a belief system in your physical mind that you can be hurt.

The term 'disease' means dis-ease with one's self. So when you hold on to all the emotions that you should have expressed or did not let go, you create heavy or lower frequencies within your body. These lower frequencies can cause havoc within your body. Instead of a cell being replaced with a new vibrant cell, it is replaced with the same lower energy vibration. It is unfortunately unable to renew itself until the history of emotions being held is released. You often hear of the saying, *'I just can't let it go'*. There comes a point when we do not want to carry a certain weight anymore. We then need to fully experience the emotions attached to the history of experiences, and through greater understanding, we can truly let things go.

Some people may wish to experience illness as an opportunity to remind themselves that they can heal their own body. Humanity is still choosing on a conscious level to have the experience of illness. It can be used as a life theme for some. It can be learning about loss for someone else. Others may use illness as a trigger moment to start living their remaining time fully in the moment and not in the past. Another may use illness to demonstrate courage or strength. Some use illness to portray a victim role.

Do you see how one word can be experienced in a variety of ways? And these mentioned are just a few.

Within us we have two avenues from which we unconsciously and consciously react: a fear-based reality with a primal instinctive feeling of protecting yourself from harm, and the other reactive way is of a love-based reality. Love is our truest state of being. This is what we are made from and who we will be forever. We are love; that is our divine birthright. You would then see the others around you in a different light and see that they too are acting from their minds and not their true state of being love.

Love cancels fear

Fear has been formed by you also to protect yourself. Love cancels fear and when we awaken to see others as ourselves, and that any wrongdoings have come from a fear-based mentality, forgiveness occurs naturally. Through the benefit of Time, we have the opportunity to correct our shortcomings and bring forth truth.

When you are afraid and fearful, you are being deceived and your mind is not operating from your spiritual higher self. Your mind is operating in judgement and you need to refocus. Your body only reacts to your mind's mis-thoughts; your body is a device for the mind to learn from, and fear is really nothing as it does not exist. Again, this concept has been created by you. Conversely, to live in a state of love is to connect with the essence of everything.

Whenever you have moments of fear, acknowledge those thoughts and say, *'Thank you for showing me what I do not prefer.'* Then decide on a new thought.

We have been given free will on this planet and an endless opportunity to experience anything we wish for. That is why there is such a diversity of human experiences, challenges, extraordinary events and situations. There are no limitations as to what we can experience or create, and no two people are the same. They may have similar things happen; however, no two individuals will experience life the exact same way. Each person has their own interpretation of events and situations, creating their experience.

Because of this freedom to choose, you determine what everything means to you – what life means to you and what certain circumstances will mean to you. That means you determine what you get out of an experience and what effect it has on you. Everything in your life reflects what you have projected out to experience for the purpose of your learning more about yourself.

My purpose in sharing this is not to burden you with guilt, but to make the point that how you view your experiences is everything. Nothing contains a meaning until you give it a meaning. Thus you can find inner peace, no matter your circumstances, simply by placing a different meaning on your experience. You are currently doing and experiencing this right now in every second of every day. This is your birthright as a human being on this planet.

> *.... you can find inner peace ... simply by placing a different meaning on your experience.*

You can turn any situation in your life into a positive experience, even if the situation may appear negative at first. It can still be viewed as positive if you choose. You just have to run with the thought that no matter what happens to you in your life, it will only serve you in a positive way, and it will.

So imagine applying this understanding of only receiving everything in a positive way to everyone in your life. Imagine being able to accept others' opinions and views even if they are different to yours. Would you be able to understand others better with accepting that their belief systems are different to yours and that they are forming their own opinions? That there is no right or wrong in this life, just many perspectives?

The world would surely be a different, and better, place.

Acknowledging the differences in life would be allowing Creation or Source to express all of itself in every possible way and without judgement. You cannot deny one thing and accept another as everything makes up the living experiences. You have been taught that there must be a right way and a wrong way. This is not so. There are just choices made at any given moment in your life with many different outcomes. Do not judge for if you judge, you are focusing on one direction.

If you come from a non-judgemental state,
you allow all possibilities to exist.

'Good' and 'bad' is subjective; it varies from person to person according to a person's perspective and relationship to what is happening. Remember that life is fundamentally neutral and that the events in your life do not begin with the concept of this is good and this is bad. Nothing in your life holds any inherent built-in meanings; you ultimately decide what it means for you. It is your relationship to the things and events in your life, your choice of perspective and belief systems, that will determine how you perceive and react to experiences. It is you that gives meaning to everything in your reality according to your beliefs.

Take for example a simple experience of rain. It rains one day. The farmer sees it as a blessing because he's been praying for rain, but a bride sees it as a disaster as it is her wedding day. So which perspective is true? Well, they are both correct. The rain will always form and fall down on the planet Earth, yet it will have a different meaning for different people. We experience and label all events according to our individual perspective.

So remember, ask yourself when you are choosing anything if it is from a love-based reality or a fear-based reality. You get to choose.

Chapter Summary

- *Fear stifles progression.*
- *Love is who you truly are.*
- *Mind and emotions play a big role in creating the world around you.*
- *Non-judgement keeps you in the flow of life.*

10

Creating Your Life

Before choosing to take incarnation and be on this planet Earth, you chose certain life themes. You basically chose an overriding theme for your life, for example, victim, survivor, teacher, rescuer, abuser and so on. You will also experience aspects of other life themes during the one life.

Take for example a life theme of being a victim. You experience your life through the eyes of a victim; however, in time you realise that you are a survivor. Then you decide to share and teach others about your experiences. Now you are a teacher. The initial theme may have been for you to experience being a victim, but the other life themes can be experienced as well.

Remember that I said all events are neutral; it is the meaning we give to our experiences that makes them what they are. With growing awareness you can start to react differently to circumstances. You get held up in traffic and you stay calm; you get overcharged but sort it out in a friendly manner. You get involved in a car accident and it's not your fault, but you are only concerned for the other person as they have never felt the care or compassion that you show them. Do you see that our emotions are determined by how we choose to experience our situations?

It is essential to understand *that life is not experienced coming at us. Life is experienced through us.*

Your entire existence is in a constant state of manifesting. You are doing this all the time, but you are not consciously aware of all the thoughts as all the possibilities are existing all at once. You don't have to wait for your circumstances to change. It is all about choosing which state you want to be in and being in a receptive state of allowing it to manifest.

It is like a radio tower sending out all the different frequencies at the same time. It is up to you as to which radio station you wish to listen to. Choose your state of being first and then allow

> *It is impossible to perceive something until you resonate with the vibration of it.*

the Universe to reflect back to you what you prefer. If you don't like what you are experiencing, you must change first before your reality can change. Become conscious of what you are manifesting for yourself. We are always believing in something; it just depends on what it is. Remember, believing is seeing, not seeing is believing. It is impossible to perceive something until you resonate with the vibration of it.

Choose to live in the state of what you really want, and faithfully hold that knowingness in your heart, allowing it to manifest for you. It is that simple! It does not have to be hard. You have been programmed to believe that everything must be difficult otherwise you cannot get what you desire. Or it won't come to you. This idea is not so. Some things can come easily. You must live as if everything is already here first. Feel it. Once you have conceived it, it already exists in the ethers. Creation always gives you what you want, and most of the time you are not aware of your own thoughts.

You were graced with creative powers for a purpose. Stop waiting for things and situations to turn up before you believe it's the other way around.

Your guidance system

We humans have access to an amazing guidance system – our enthusiasm. This is our higher selves speaking to our non-physical selves. It's showing us the way. It is saying to keep doing what you are doing. This is your higher soul consciousness in communication with you. If you know what you want to manifest, that's great. Otherwise just learn to check in with yourself and ask a simple question: *Is this what I am most enthusiastic about?* Is your enthusiasm high? Is this decision the next best thing you can think of?

Following your highest enthusiasm is all that is required. Use this as the radar and rudder of your own ship whenever you want to manifest something. If you have not decided on what you want, maybe it's because the necessary pieces of information may not have found you yet. So when certain things come to you, you are then able to make your decision. The most important thing is your state of being and how you feel. Remember, all the possibilities exist simultaneously.

Imagine a long line with all your choices and simply picking what you want. Everything is in the non-physical yet everything that you can imagine exists here and now. All that is required is to think about something, picturing yourself in that experience, and imagining what it feels like, holding that vibration and living as if it has already happened. Then the Universe will do all its magic to manifest it for you.

Please remember that changing your mind every two seconds will get you nowhere. The Universe will give you nothing as you do not know what you prefer or really want. So it is important to give some clarification and focus on the things that you desire, so that there is a clear direction and path for the Universe to follow. What you put out is what you will receive. This is Universal Law.

It will help if you can relax and go with the flow, trusting in doing things that you may have not done before and being willing to go an extra mile. Don't resist the flow no matter what it looks like. *The only reason people find it hard is that they are insisting on how things should go, or be, or form, or when things should come.* If you do this, you are putting expectations on the very thing that you want, instead of allowing and trusting Creation to manifest in its own way. Sometimes it has a quicker route than you think of.

Sometimes your mind or ego tells you certain things as it does not know how things are meant to come to you. It is important to start listening to your mind less and start becoming heartfelt. *Your mind can only compute what is going on in the moment.* It does not know how or when things are coming, so it turns to fear as it does not know any better. The ego is there to keep you focused on your physical reality. When you start listening to the mind chatter, you are allowing yourself to believe the ego is right and you are letting the mind rule your life. The ego is there for focus and survival, not for you to decide on your thinking. Your desires have already been sent to Creation and it already has a path laid out. Creation has matched your vibration, so relax and let the Universe do what it always has done: manifest your desire for you into physicality.

You may sometimes receive the opposite to what you want. Well, it just might be because you are unintentionally or unconsciously believing in the opposite of what you really want. You see, Creation will give you exactly what you are wishing for. It could be that you say one thing but are really believing something else to be true. And it's your highest belief of something, so that is what will be manifested. Your belief system plays an especially important role. Something that you must become very conscious of.

So if there are things about your reality that you want to change, it can be done. Since reality is experienced through the inner self, *redefine your situation.* Change your thoughts inside you then see the change on the outside. The situation may stay the same, but it does not mean that you have to experience it the same way. Change your thoughts and you will experience things differently.

The physical world around you that you see is simply a reflection of you. If you see happiness around you, chances are you are happy, or the reflection is saying be happy if you are not. The same thing goes if you are unhappy. You may be seeing unhappiness around you. At that point you can check in within yourself and ask, 'Am I unhappy?' If so, the only person who can change is you.

It is so important to *believe in your desire*. Eventually there will be no more doubt and only certainty in the quest for what you desire. You don't have to do anything at all if you have a strong belief already. Just live in the expectancy that things will arrive when they are supposed to. The Universe is never late; it will always give you everything you need.

What I have explained are guidelines for you to follow in manifesting the things and situations for your life. It's about surrendering to Source for it knows the right path for you, and not over thinking things. You may experience some challenging times in your life, but why not give them a new meaning? 'What belief system am I carrying that means I am viewing this moment this way?' You may find that it is all in your mind.

When I became homeless, I had a choice. How I was going to navigate through that experience was up to me. I could have seen it as a negative experience. Instead, I chose to transform it, to learn from it, to grow from it, to enrich myself. Was it challenging? Yes, at times. But I had to trust and believe in Source. Something that I had experienced many times over before in my life.

Like I did, you will learn more about yourself. All you'll have to do is change your point of view and beliefs and you will experience something entirely new from the situation. These trials and tribulations and tests are allowing you the opportunity to see the many sides of your consciousness that you were not aware of before. This then allows you the opportunity to choose what you prefer and what you don't want.

Situations may look like they are going against you, but in fact they are there merely pointing you to a new direction. You are experiencing your reality through your eyes. Take responsibility for the world you are creating.

Rewrite the script

Where necessary, rewrite the script you are telling yourself. Create your reality effortlessly, allowing yourself to experience 100 percent trust in knowing that the Universe will fully

> *Where necessary, rewrite the script you are telling yourself.*

support you in the reality you truly desire to experience. When you are aligned with the Universe in this way, the synchronicity is astounding! Things will appear to fall into place effortlessly.

When life looks like it is falling apart, have the perspective that maybe your life is falling *together* for the first time. You may be releasing all the things that no longer serve you. Disappointments are only temporary; it is your thoughts that make things appear permanent. Even frustrations are just the result of you thinking about things in a wrong way. Try focusing on the things you do want instead of the things you don't want. Remember, *your thoughts create your reality, so take a serious look at what you are creating.*

The word 'imagination' is often frowned upon, yet it is a special key. It not only gives you ideas; it also shows you all the different possibilities. How many times have you heard this?

'Get your head out of the clouds.'

'Oh that child has a vivid imagination.'

'Stop daydreaming. Get back to reality.'

Hello world! Have you ever stopped to think that imagination is a gateway to your higher self and a medium for communication? New inventions are conceived by people using their creative imagination. The same goes for painters and sculptors who create masterpieces and those who devise new businesses and find solutions to problems.

It's time to go to that place of silence within yourself.

Let yourself dream.

Let yourself be immersed in all the possibilities life has to offer. Dream a dream and make it big, for you cannot outdream the dream the Universe has for you.

You can't make a dream come true unless you dream of it first.

Your higher self knows what you want to manifest, and it sometimes appears that what you want does not happen when you want it to. This is because of your expectations and the timeframes you impose. Maybe the path you are on is required for you to meet certain people or require certain skills, to progress further. It may be for you to exercise patience – even to teach you about faith and trust. When you eventually do get what you want, you will then appreciate it in a way that you never thought possible. Timing is everything. If a dream is stillborn (manifested too early) it has no savour. Acknowledge and respect that the higher self knows the correct timing for everything and trust that the Universe is never late.

Let's look at an example of a projected movie script you may be giving yourself.

You live in an apartment, but your belief system says, 'I really want a house'. So now you have two versions of reality going on. Your physical reality is you living in an apartment. But your mind and heart keep seeing and believing in a house, which is in the non-physical reality.

You must hold the thought that you are in a house, which is a different frequency and vibration, and then the Universe has to give you your belief system. The energy you give out and what you focus on will be the experience.

The outer reality is a reflection of the inner belief systems that you carry.

You and the house were always there in a non-physical state. It is up to you to turn your attention from your present (physical) situation and re-focus it instead on the version of you and the house that exists in the (non-physical) ethers through your creative imagination. You are changing something that already exists in the non-physical into physical form. The more you focus on a thought (which holds its own vibration) the more you will see it come to form, for it already exists. You must let go of the non-preferred reality and focus on the preferred reality, and your senses will shift and change accordingly.

Every time you change reality, it is not through your physical body but rather that your consciousness is shifting into another body that already exists in that new reality. You technically do not have to create anything.

It's about selecting what you prefer and allowing it into your life.

It's also especially important to remember that Creation will have its own timing to deliver your wishes. It knows exactly when, where and what you need at precisely the right time, and not a moment too early nor too late.

You are using three aspects of yourself:

1. *Mental* – You picture, or see, what you want. You have to see it, imagine, dream and see all the details of what you what.
2. *Emotional* – Once you have a firm picture, then you have to *feel* (the heart). Creating your desire is a collaborative work of heart and mind. Using your creative imagination, picture yourself in the moment in what you desire, using all your senses. Get excited and passionate about your dream!
3. *Being* – The final step is just *being it*. Act as if you have your desire. It is already here – a fait accompli.

When you understand the process you will see that you are like a light beam of consciousness going from one body to another body in each reality. In the above example, we see physical 3D consciousness shifting its attention to the mental body and then focusing attention on the emotional body when the heart is brought into play. This is your consciousness shifting to the parallel body in the appropriate new reality you are focusing on.

At this 3D level, things must play out sequentially. There is a saying – 'One thing at a time'. From the non-physical perspective everything appears all at once, the whole story. It is only when physically experienced that 'the whole story' is spread apart, made to appear distant from one thing to another and drawn out in a lengthy way.

Chapter Summary

- *Life does not 'happen' to you. It is experienced through you.*
- *You have to match the vibration of something for it to manifest.*
- *Your thoughts can be facilitating your progress or impeding it.*
- *Enthusiasm is key to manifesting your desire.*
- *You can re-write your script at any time.*

11

Time and Space

Time and space are an illusion. The perception of time is formed by the collective consciousness. It's your consciousness constantly shifting again to different points of view. The so-called 'empty space' that you see is full of different structures. You cannot perceive them as you are not of that same vibration. In other dimensions they would be projecting out their own perceptions that are real to them. You see, all physical matter is just constructions and we are connected to the physical matter that we see.

If you look at the whole Earth, we are individuals, yet we make up part of the whole construct. There are many particles that make up the whole. Imagine if one particle were to shift or move – it would affect the rest. The physical planet is solidified thought created from the inner and projected outward. Time and space are the perceptions of your physical senses and chosen beliefs. You are just focusing on one dimension of reality, yet other realities exist in the same precise area. You simply blot them out.

> *Time and space are the perceptions of your physical senses and chosen beliefs.*

Depending on what space you are in, your thoughts are interchangeable. For example, the same space where physical matter is may appear as light or even sound in another plane. So, the same space that you can see may have ten layers. But you are only seeing the physical through your physical eyes. If you were to focus your attention upon your non-physical senses, you would then become aware of the other dimensions existing. This is a basic understanding or a platform for you to begin with.

The five physical senses deal with physical reality and the inner senses deal with realities that are holographic in nature. The other realities are *hidden* within you because you are so focused on the physical that you are not aware of the other layers that exist. Each layer has its own frequency. These layers either appear as a solid structure or they are holographic.

Your oversoul and your subconscious

Subconsciousness is the go-between for the mind and the brain. It bridges the inner and outer senses. Once you begin the journey of expanding into other realms, your awareness grows. Not all of yourself is contained in the body that you know of as yourself. There is another component – your higher self. Your physical consciousness is just a portion of your true identity. The higher self (oversoul) does not live in a time space reality. The other portions of your identity are also having experiences elsewhere, even on other planets.

Time does not exist in the non-physical. When consciousness relates to physical form, it sees things as a sequence of events. Therefore, it compares one moment to another and we have labelled it as 'time'. This labelling comes from a physical perspective. There is only one moment seen from different perspectives over and over again. A movie reel is made up of many tiny frames. Yet when you see them moving quickly it looks like motion. The same for our existence. We see movement, but it is just one moment repeated after another, appearing like everything is moving, and we get the experience of movement.

Just as your soul and body go hand in hand, you have a consciousness attached to your body. As mentioned, this is just a part of your oversoul (the higher dimensional self) that exists in the non-physical. You are also having other lifetimes as we speak. Let's say your oversoul wishes to have an experience of living in France in the 18th Century, of living in the 20th Century and living on a different planetary system. It can be done because a portion of the oversoul is conscious in all those lifetimes. This is why when you picture yourself in different lifetimes, you are tapping into your oversoul.

Expanding on this, you are having more than one lifetime at once. You are currently on Earth and yet other portions of your oversoul are elsewhere, maybe as another person or even on other planets. When you open up your awareness, you are tapping into the other portions of your oversoul. Remember, each lifetime has a personality and consciousness all of its own, with its own frequency.

Every thought and physical thing that you see is fundamentally energy. We each carry a signature vibration or frequency – our very own refection of Source. When we merge down into a physical expression, we create a vibration of physical DNA of that expression and it is also recorded in a non-physical expression that belongs to you. Your DNA information will hold many lifetimes, but not all DNA is turned on to each new lifetime. So when you wish to discover your origins, you may discover that it is not from the one planet or even one specific race. All the information of all your existences in the non-physical realm is held and recorded by you. There is nothing you cannot access. All the experiences that you choose to create add to the expansion of your individual consciousness. For this information to be accessed, you must turn your attention within, as the answers are inside you. Be willing to understand the data you are seeing and receiving, and what it represents and means.

Frequencies and reality

There is not one thing in the Universe that does not have a frequency. You are a frequency along with everything you see – every blade of grass, ant, tree, star .... the whole Universe. When enough conscious attention is given to something it creates matter. This is called the 'observer consciousness'. Each individual is creating a personal reality and when combined with others, it forms another frequency – the collective reality. That then produces another frequency of its own.

All frequencies can be interpreted as numerical values and are mathematically observable This means that one can mathematically predict interactions between objects and situations. With this understanding one can make a blueprint of a small location or a big star map to guide spaceships through the Universe.

When we look at our reality, the concept of time has been created by us by looking at a clock or using a calendar. However, this concept has been formed from an Earthly

> *Reality is just a series of different pictures that look like motion.*

perspective. Reality is just one moment. You see the experience of time as passing moments and they are all physiological. Reality is just a series of different pictures that look like motion.

Let's use the analogy of a clock. There are 60 seconds to a minute. Let's break it up into moments. Each moment is the same moment expressed and experienced from a different point of view. The world is a stationary stage, while the moments in our day are constantly changing. Every moment that ticks over is a new moment containing a new past, a new present moment and a new future. All the possibilities of everything that you could choose exists in every new moment.

Imagine that 60 seconds as a short film. The film has been made and you want to look at it. You would find that the one-minute film consists of small still frames (the moments), but when you put it through a movie reel it looks like it has motion. You are making the movie every moment and you are deciding how the movie goes. You the actor are in all the movies you are creating. You exist in all the possible movies that you can think of.

Once you become aware that you are the rudder of your own ship, you realise that everything you have ever experienced on Earth is one moment in Creation. The same moment that is recreated from a different perspective, repeatedly. You create the past, future and present from the here and now. From the one moment you imagine a future moment and reflect on a moment before and you label this the past and future.

There is only one moment, and that is the now. You think that there is time and space; that is the illusion created by consciousness. Everything is formed from the now, and what you are experiencing right now is the physicality of one life. All the other life themes past and future exist all at the same time as well.

Every moment is a new moment and is slightly different from the previous moment. It's a new version of Earth. You may think that because you can remember events and circumstances that this is your past. This recall is Creation stored from the fabric of Creation itself. No matter what Universe or galaxy you are occupying, its structure is formed by the same material. So, you can obtain any moments in time from anywhere because it is held suspended and imprinted into the same atoms that form everything. You are not only part of the whole; you are also the whole itself. All information is suspended in Creation, yet anyone can obtain that information, as we are Creation.

We view life on this planet as a linear line. Consider this concept instead: a picture, a grid of lines forming a square cube with lifetime positions in various places within that cube. This would be a little different to what you are used to. Are you able to grasp this? What if I were to say you can go back in 'time' and change the past? I am not saying you can go back and physically take on that form, as you are choosing this moment to be you whatever that form is now. However, you can go back with your mind and soul and connect to your 'past life' and get more out of it. Experience it again and change the past.

I am talking about *creating other timelines for yourself.*

You may have had a bad experience as a child and as an adult you find that others involved are still living and you don't have anything to do with them or they may have died. Here is what you can do: Go back mentally to that time and place and relive that moment. Allow yourself to feel all the emotions that that event gives you. Now, look at the moment from the other peoples' perspective. Did they know any better? Were they aware of their actions? Did they know how you were feeling at the time? Did they even care? Did you feel like the victim?

There are two parts to this message. I am referring firstly to the perspective of the other people and your involvement. Let's look at an example. You were young, you were defenceless, and your power was taken away from you in a particular experience. You now can forgive yourself for wanting to experience the lack of power. Later in life you have come to realise that you have all power, and it is time to regain your power. Tell that child inside yourself that it wasn't your fault and not to feel guilty.

Secondly, about the other parties involved, just as you created another timeline for yourself, you can do the same for them. By seeing things from a different perspective, you have already created a different timeline that the other people may experience also. Through this on another level you can provide the opportunity for them to experience being forgiven. Whether they are alive or passed over, those new thoughts are still able to influence the other parties involved.

Remember that all thoughts are energy, so you can imagine for both parties involved. The energies may have been dark and painful, but by taking on a different perspective you will be inviting higher, more loving frequencies to all parties involved. Everyone benefits and all become receivers. A healing takes place. So give it a try and release any pain. We tend to carry around too much baggage. So travel light and be well and healthy.

Chapter Summary

- *Everything carries a frequency.*
- *Frequency match determines your dimensional experience.*
- *You create past, present and future in the here and now.*
- *You can create a new timeline for yourself to change a past bad experience.*

12

Wake Up to Who You Are

In knowing who you truly are, it's important to let go of this idea of 'normal'. What is normal? Why has humanity chosen to categorise people into a particular slot? Perhaps it makes some people feel better, so they can say, 'Oh I am normal' or 'She is not normal'. This makes some people feel better about themselves. Maybe we categorise others because we are unable to understand them. For some, it's easier to just judge.

There is no 'normal'. How boring would it be? Let's just say there is variety. Some people may be similar in some things or think the same way, but does it matter if someone doesn't fit in with what you believe in? Does it matter that they don't like you? This world is not made up of everything being all the same. We are all human, but we have chosen to take on different forms and personalities. If it weren't for these differences, we would not have the opportunity to see our individuality. Yet on another level we as individuals are part of the whole and that whole is unlimited by nature.

Creation is experiencing itself from a particular point of view through you. No other person will ever experience life the way you see it. When you think about the whole concept, it is amazing. You are so unique and special to be who you are now. Be kind to yourself and love yourself for your individuality, no matter what form it comes in.

Have you ever thought of looking at the differences on Earth as the perfect opportunity for changing yourself? Every change we make creates a difference for humanity. The differences you see are a perfect opportunity to determine your preferences, your likes and dislikes. If there are some things or situations you want to change, then go for it.

It does not matter how things are going to come about. Creation always has a plan. You just have to decide for change, believing in what you want to change. The laws of Creation will *always* give you what you believe. *Your brain is like a computer – data in data out.* It can only process what it has been taught and experienced. It acts like a library, processing your life like a book. Someone must write the book, and you are writing the book. Your life is forming the pages of the book, and your brain is processing all the data using your physical senses.

Your brain does not know how things are going to come about. It will try to convince you that you don't have the money, don't have the contacts, you are not brainy enough, what's required is way out of your reach…

Do not live by your brain. You live under the laws of Creation and what you want exists if you truly believe it is possible

Creation will always give you what you believe and want to experience. Each thought and emotion carry its own electromagnetic current, being totally unique. We could be compared to transformers, unconsciously creating advanced electromagnetic units into physical objects all around us. You are experiencing the world from a reflection of your inner reality. You are the same as the very atoms that make up a table, a tree, a tomato and even an animal. All consciousness comes together as one into the forms you perceive.

Form is not permanent

There is also another essential notion to understand: form is not permanent. This is an illusion as all consciousness is always in a state of change. Every moment is a new moment. Your atoms and molecules are constantly changing, dying and being replaced. So your physical body that you have now is different to the previous moment.

Your physical body defines the structure of who you are, but you cannot use your physical senses alone to understand the true nature of who you are. You must use your non-physical senses (intuition and inner sight) to perceive the other dimensions and realities and communicate with your higher non-physical mind. There is always some sort of communication going on, but most people are totally unaware that this is happening. When these aspects are brought to light and the physical and non-physical senses can work in harmony together, how you experience your 3D physical world will change forever.

You and I are projections from our higher selves into physical reality, acting out different situations and moments to have a physical experience. You are the physicality of Creation expressing itself with free will and manifesting anything you could possibility imagine. Yet you have been given the experience to be an individual and still be a part of the whole.

There is a percentage of humanity who are choosing to no longer experience life through the negative perspective, rather choosing different timelines. All the possibilities exist simultaneously. You don't have to wait for your circumstances to change or wait to

> *It is all about choosing which state of being you want to experience and allowing the Universe to give to you.*

win the jackpot. It is all about choosing which state of being you want to experience and allowing the Universe to give to you.

It is like a radio station. All the frequencies exist at the same time. It is up to you as to which radio station you wish to listen to, or in human terms which reality you wish to experience. It's about choosing your state of being first, then allowing the Universe to reflect to you your belief system. And if you don't like what you are experiencing, you must then choose again before the reality can change again. We are always believing in something. It just depends on what it is. Remember, you are deciding.

You must believe first, for believing is seeing not seeing is believing.

If all of humanity was to take a leap of faith and believe first, and live in the state of being that it has already been given to them, how relaxed would everyone be! There would be less worry and fear. Here is the irony: Creation gives all your wishes whether you are aware of what you are wanting or not. So it's your time to wake up to who you really are, and what you are capable of.

So who are you?

Your whole reason for being on this planet Earth is to awaken to remember who you are, your origins. This is all being done through the infinite possibilities that you can create.

You are in essence spirit or life force in a physical form, which we could call energy. This energy has so much power and consciousness, having the ability to create and experience whatever it wishes. You have created yourself out of the unified field of consciousness of energy that makes up everything through investing a certain amount of focus and attention. This is why you have actualized, and your body has an awareness of itself. You can physically touch it.

The same energy that you are made up of makes up the other people, objects and animals you see around you. So your consciousness is made up of the 'you' that you know, and you are everybody else as well. Altogether we make the whole. There is no difference from you or anything else that you see around you. It's all energy in some sort of form; we are everything.

Earth possesses the structure for you to experience limitations, suffering and darkness for you to experience the light and expand your consciousness as to who you really are. Both experiences of dark and light are as equally as important. They both exist and you will experience both aspects in any given lifetime.

Limitations are illusions. What appears as limitations are only opportunities for you to expand to become whole. Suffering and limitation is self-imposed, leading to separation from Source and loss of self-love.

You can integrate all these different perspectives and accept them as part of your whole self. Love is the key! Take full responsibility for your creation. If you are experiencing it, you have created it. You can dissolve all suffering by facing your problems with an understanding of opposites, or duality. Possibility dwells in opposing forces (polarity) and the answer may be found within the possibility that opposites present. With time and patience, opposites can be transcended and integrated into a situation in a way that makes things work.

Death will appear when you choose to no longer have a physical body. You constructed the appearance of the physical body and you gave yourself a personality, thinking that it is real until death approaches and your focus of attention is directed elsewhere. After you die you go back initially to the astral plane at the level of awakened consciousness that you carried when in the body, choosing your experiences now on the other side. You do not fully integrate back to Source. If you did, you would no longer be in a reincarnate situation.

Beings at the level of Source are, of course, non-physical and are omniscient (all-knowing). They abide in oneness rather than singularity. Many people will continue to choose reincarnation for the purposes of awakening. The desire to return to Earth ceases when the planet can no longer further their spiritual growth.

Remember, there are many people with different levels of awareness. So a person experiencing a limited amount of consciousness would see their lifetime purely as just a physical body with no afterlife. Someone with a higher degree of awareness would be experiencing life on Earth in a much more expanded way. They would know that they are spirit creating and projecting through a physical form, and that the current lifetime does not define all of them.

Even though there is an ego attached to the physical body, they are not ruled and governed by it. They know and see everyone as equal, understanding that the common bond that unites them is Creation expressing itself in different ways. This is an awakened person.

We are not aware of all the realities that exist. The higher the degree of awareness, the closer we return to being one with all.

*Earth is designed to separate us from Source, and
the return and restoration of consciousness to source
is the goal and purpose of our existence.*

Everyone has a story

We all have a story to tell. Our interpretation of our experiences forms our reality and how we view our world. Your life is a form, an aspect, of Creation, and every moment of your existence is a continual progression of learning and experience. Even when you have acquired a certain amount or level of knowledge, your life will only bring you more opportunities to further expand, and some will be quite challenging. There will be countless questions you will ask yourself. There will be love and tears, and you will see the lightness and darkness of the world you live in. My point here is that you will see the world in duality as it is in the abyss that your greatest learning can take place. Experiencing the opposite of what you want gives you the opportunity to define what you truly prefer.

Relationships also provide the most incredible learning experiences to define what you prefer. They can be tricky and challenging at times. You can find yourself in situations that evoke intense emotions. The main purpose of relationships is to give you the opportunity to know yourself better, to perceive and refine the attributes and beliefs systems that you carry.

Our soul family or 'tribe' are often closer than our birth family. It is whoever we most identify with – those who have been placed in our path perhaps (for example, through adoption or fostering) who provide the foundations for our chosen life theme before we took incarnation. So when we look at one someone else, we should not be too judgemental. Everyone has a reason for choosing their situation for their own growth.

We encounter so many relationships over a lifetime – some are fleeting moments, some weeks, some years. It does not matter how short or long as all interactions will hold some sort of experience for you. Not only can your long-standing close relationships give you profound growth as an individual soul, but even your briefest encounters with total strangers can make a huge impact on your life as well. Embrace all people and walks of life because you never know what the next person you meet might do for you or, more importantly, what you might learn from them. Thank everyone who has ever turned up in your life for you would not have become who you are without them.

Not everyone will be feeling happy all the time. Sometimes people just don't want to deal with how they are feeling. But how you handle these feelings and how it affects others is your responsibility. You need to acknowledge your feelings, but it would be irresponsible to pour your baggage onto the next person you come across. The emotions you feel are yours, not someone's else responsibility to deal with, especially anger.

Self-awareness

Most importantly find and strengthen your relationship with yourself. Get to know yourself. Don't be a stranger to yourself. Go to the very depths of your being and find out who you really are. Spend precious moments looking after yourself. Only then can you give the best version of you out to the world. And maybe then the relationships

> *Find and strengthen your relationship with yourself.*

in your life will grow and change to reflect the new you. Ultimately, the first relationship should be with yourself as you are the first person you are consciously aware of.

You wake up and you see you have a body. You are the first thing that you truly acknowledge, so make knowing yourself a priority. We are seldom taught that. Rather, we are made to feel guilty to think of ourselves. We sometimes hurt ourselves without even realising it. Everything in your life is your choice and for your experience, whether you are conscious of your manifestations or not.

If you are someone who is used to always doing what others say, and not listening in to your own inner voice and following it, it can feel a little weird at first to start not giving a damn about what others think. You might think you are being selfish. But my point here is not to encouragement selfishness that hurts others but to really be true to yourself, and what you are here for, by listening within. In doing so, you may be doing something new. It's like you have just unlocked some invisible chains that were keeping you from being your authentic self. If there is a version of yourself that you would like to become, then do it. Do whatever it takes and believe that anything is possible.

You may think of your soul as something that you can contain or put into something. Well, your soul or whatever you want to call it is not of this concept. It is alive and well, forever changing. Your consciousness forms the body that you know yourself as being. It also has an awareness of itself before the body and after losing the body as well. This perception of awareness that the soul carries always exists. It will never die. The experiences that you create add to what makes up your soul.

Your soul will project out to the world the necessary ideas for it to learn, and you will sometimes find yourself in the same types of situations until you get the correct learning that your soul needs to experience. Everything that happens to you is for your benefit. You get to understand more about yourself and the different ideas that you are carrying within yourself.

Remember, life is experienced through you not at you. An awakened person does not play the blame game. There is no room for self-pity. It is about being responsible for everything that you think is happening to you and finding the lesson and experience you have chosen to experience in this lifetime.

Chapter Summary

- *Creation is experiencing itself from a particular point of view through you.*
- *Differences are an opportunity to determine what you prefer.*
- *You are energy with power and consciousness.*
- *Experiences of both light and dark are necessary.*
- *Know yourself and develop an awareness of your inner life.*

13

The Future

We are the change; we the people of this Earth are the future. YOU are the change. As I mentioned throughout this book, the future is always the manifestation of the now moment of our current thoughts and beliefs. So to say one specific thing or things might happen isn't correct. It would only be one probability as there are countless alternatives that must be factored in. Which timeline are you going to be on, and which perspective will have your greatest focus and attention? These are the things that will determine your future. As I have said, nothing is set in stone as we all have free will to change our minds in every moment.

However, the awakening process that I and thousands of other good people around the world have been experiencing has provided a new expansion of waking consciousness and awareness. Our thinking of what and who we are, what we deserve and how we are supposed to live has changed. My vision for the world is clear. I, along with many others, no longer wish for anyone to be defined or controlled. I envision a unification of oneness in which we can all express ourselves, yet know we are all part of the whole. I look to a world in which we have the freedom to choose and express ourselves without condemnation.

Freedom will mean that everyone will have access to basic food and water and shelter, thus eliminating hunger and starvation on this planet. Our future freedom also means the release of new free energy and new technologies and full global acceptance of natural medical healing modalities such as cannabis oil, essential oils and ancient herbs. Our schools should be places of excitement where children can choose their topics of interests and learn at their own pace. Freedom means an education system that encourages each individual's talents, skills and interests, instead of wanting everybody to be the same. Imagine how many Einsteins the world would create in an education system where there was freedom to grow without limitations!

We most certainly need to restructure our government departments, for the current system is not representing the views of the people and displaying an open and transparent operation. New and improved systems must be introduced for our future to move forward.

Change is the one constant that the world experiences daily, so let's be more conscious of the changes that we each make. Just like a stone that can be thrown into a river or pond, making ripples that can touch the water's edge, we the people are the same. Our energies can touch one another and influence someone else's aura just by our presence alone.

Our Love should be the currency in this world, not greed and crime.

I believe that our Mother Earth has been telling us through natural disasters to look at ourselves and how we have been treating her. Many of us are listening and becoming recycling kings and queens where possible. Nature wants us to stop using pesticides and chemicals that poison our Earth and deplete her of her goodness.

It is time for humanity to focus on being of service to others rather than a 'what can I get out of this' kind of attitude. As a self-focused culture, we have forgotten that all are our brothers and sisters, and we should be helping each other. The vision is in the words of John Lennon's song, 'To unite as one, to think as one', for it is time for us to unite.

This unity includes our animal kingdom. Cruelty to animals has got to stop around the world. We are co-existing with the animal kingdom, yet we have abused and mistreated many species on our planet. We are meant to be stewards, and the brotherhood of a New Earth will be a brotherhood of all the kingdoms of Nature. All Creation will live in perfect co-existence.

The need for change has come and we are currently going through a great awakening. Some refer to it as the second coming of Christ Consciousness. It does not matter what one calls it. This is a transformation of the inner, of the soul remembering its connection to Source. It does not matter your race or nationality; we have all come from Source and will return to Source.

Transformation is the process of stopping to look outside of yourself and looking within. It is living in a more conscious state of awareness. It is taking responsibility for your actions and the energy you give out. It is the shift in awareness from the physical to the non-physical planes.

Every moment of your existence is an opportunity for spiritual growth. It does not matter what you are doing, or where you are. When you are on a yacht, a cliff of a mountain, sitting on a grassed hill in a park, knitting a scarf in a rocking chair, cooking your favourite meal ... your consciousness is with you wherever you go.

Awakening is about becoming aware of the given moment and the thoughts you are having. Is it the best thing that you could be doing for the day? Is this moment making you happy and fulfilled? Or is it challenging you in some way? How you are viewing your moment will be how you experience it. Your attitude and perspective determine everything.

Living light

If your mind and your heart are saying two different things, ask yourself: *Which one will I follow? Why? Which side will I show the world? Why?*

What living light am I going to show for someone else to follow? When? How?

What does 'living light' mean to me?

How can I guard and nurture this living light?

What would be the outcome if we all reflected living light?

Can I think of specific people who would benefit from the living light I choose to reflect? Is this living light for everyone or just some?

Are there circumstances where I would withhold reflecting this living light? If so, what are they?

What strategies can I put into place to ensure that my awakening journey continues?

What am I going to do to ensure that I can live more fully in the present moment of now?

In doing the shadow work on yourself, check into what situations make you feel uncomfortable, sad, angry or resentful. These are the moments that you need to work on. Don't deny these events or situations as they surface. Rather, by forgiving, transcending and integrating these energies you ultimately regain your power. All uncomfortable situations relate to the concept of separation and the experience of pain and suffering. Life is giving us endless possibilities for growth. Love will be the key to your existence as that is what you are.

If you feel scared about living a new way, that is okay because you are charting unfamiliar territory. I hope that by now, though, the *Awakening Teachings* have reminded you that you are much more powerful that you ever imagined. You are awakening, step by step.

Allow yourself time to experience and feel the newness of your new thoughts about yourself. You will learn gradually that it's about balancing your spirit, mind and body. When you are out of alignment with your true natural self, you will experience a feeling of not being right. This is probably because you are carrying someone else's belief systems. You see, your own belief systems will make you feel alive, light and happy. That's how you can differentiate whether you are living by your belief systems or others'.

It is so easy for others to make decisions for you. Everybody will think they know what is best for you. What would happen if you told everyone to TAKE OFF, and then got rid of all versions of what everyone thinks of you and go find who you think you want to be? Better still, go and create the version you want to show the world.

Do not be held captive to someone else's version of you.
You and you alone must take responsibility for the decisions
and actions that you make.
MAKE NEW FOOTPRINTS and create a new path.

LIGHT the world with your unique 'living light', not someone else's as NO ONE can shine the way that you can.

BE the individual that you are. There is no one else like you and no one can duplicate you.

DON'T be afraid to walk your truth and show your light.

CREATE that epiphany moment for yourself, right now if you have not already done so. You are awakening, one moment at a time.

I am honoured that you and I both chose to share this lifetime together.

Epilogue: The Extra-Terrestrials

We now live in a modern age of technology, and information is more readily available than ever before. I urge you to trust in your own guidance and learn to feel what is right for you. Do your own research. There are many people all over the planet who have had connections with beings in many ways. To say that one way or one piece of information is better than another would be to deny each its own truth or expression.

Because each of us has our own unique experience, we all can access and receive information differently. But altogether it is part of a much bigger picture.

You may be wondering, *What about the ETs?* What is their role in all of this? Can't they help?

ETs cannot be held responsible for the actions that mankind make. They can only observe and give guidance; they cannot intervene in the way you expect. This would be going against galactic laws. ETs are only able to intervene at a level of the combined consciousness of the planet they are involved with. Earth still has a lot more learning to go in the fields of spirituality and technology. Each person must be responsible for his or her actions. It is up to the humans of Earth to want to advance and evolve as a species. It would not be right for ETs to do the work and make the decisions for the Earth people. The learning must be individually done and not given on a silver platter. It is better to learn from experience.

Over time you will uncover who you are and your purpose. I now know that I am a messenger. I chose to incarnate as a human being and have had several incarnations here on Earth, returning to assist humanity to wake up from what I would call a 'sleepy state'. The Awakening is now. You have the power that you need to wake up; it resides within you.

Currently on Earth, there are three very distinct groups that make up mankind. The first group of individuals are the Cabal or Dark Forces – the governments, secret societies, people of satanic rituals and so on. These people do not have nice agendas for humanity. They wish to reduce the population and have control over the human mind and soul. They do not hold any empathy.

The second group are all the sleeping ones – those that go about their day, going to work, watching TV, thinking that the governments are there to protect them and that they follow all the rules.

Then there is a third level of humans – the star seeds, lightworkers, walk-ins – awakened and conscious beings who are here to raise the consciousness of humans and evolve Earth from a 3D state of consciousness to a 5D level of consciousness. They are here to help provide open contact with our galactic neighbours and intergalactic civilisations that already exist in our galaxy.

There is a war going on for the domination of Earth. Between the light and dark. The awakening that is occurring right now on planet Earth is about raising one's consciousness and awareness. The Dark use fear and power to control the population. They do not wish the masses to awaken. There will be a group of people that will not awaken in this lifetime. It would be too hard for them as it will be easier for them to continue to believe in the lies than to stand up to them.

The fact that you are reading this book says you are ready for change or may have already begun that change. I am awake and very conscious in my participation in raising man's consciousness and evolving Earth. Perhaps it's time for you to find your particular purpose at this time of awakening.

I will leave you with my recent message from my galactic family:

> *People of the Earth! It is your time to question what you hear from media and politicians. Don't be sheep in a herd! You have a right as a human being to know the truth. We are pointing you to a new direction, a new world for you to discover for yourself. We entreat you to take your power back and to stand in your truth.*

Bibliography and Resources

Books

Conversations with God Trilogy 3 Book; Neal Donald Walsch; Hodder and Stoughton (1 January 1 2017)

When Everything Changes Change Everything; Neal Donald Walsch; Createspace (10 March 10 2011)

A Course in Miracles; Helen Schucman and William Thetford; Foundation for Inner Peace (3rd ed. January 1, 1975)

Seth Speaks: The Eternal Validity of the Soul; Jane Roberts (notes by Robert F Butts); Amber-Allen Publ, New World Library; Reprint Edition (23 May 1994)

The Seat of the Soul; Gary Zukav; Random House (1 May 2016)

The Disappearance of the Universe; Gary R Renard; Hay House; 1st edition (1 December 2004)

Thiaoouba Prophecy; Michael Desmarquet; Arafura Publishing 2004

The Power of Now; Eckhart Tolle; New World Library (19 August 2004)

Crossing Over; John Edwards; Hay House (26 February 2004)

Don't Kiss Them Goodbye; Alison DuBois; Touchstone;
Reprint edition (1 November 1 2005)

The Unbelievable Truth; Gordon Smith; Hay House UK
(8 September 2005)

Talking to Heaven; James Van Praagh; Berkley; Reissue edition
(1 March 1999)

Born Knowing; John Holland; Hay House Inc. (1 February 2003)

Adventures of a Psychic; Silvia Brown; Hay House Inc.;
Revised, Subsequent edition (1 September 1998)

Websites
www.bashar.org – Darryl Anka channels the ET Bashar
Cosmic Agency and Gosia (YouTube)
Bentinho Massaro (YouTube)
Christine Day (YouTube)

Acknowledgements

My three beautiful children Tanisha, Brianna and Jayden. Thank you for inspiring me and making me so proud. I will always be your loving mum and be here for you.

My love William. Thank you for the unconditional love and support that you have given me and for accepting me for who I am.

Peter, the father of my children. I thank you for giving me the opportunity to experience motherhood.

My deceased parents and grandparents. Thank you for your unconditional love and for showing me what patience and strength is all about.

Thanks to my beautiful Aunty Ann and belated Uncle Leo, my second parents. You have always been there through thick and thin.

Thanks to my dear brother Sal and sister Cecelia for always being there with your guidance and support.

Thanks to all my extended family members: my in-laws, nephews and nieces and close cousins. I cherish your love and support and the momentous times we have spent together.

I also acknowledge the many close, beautiful friends in my life for not only being with me in good times but the lows as well. To my first spiritual teacher, Gay, who gave me friendship, guidance and sound spiritual knowledge. Our time together laid the foundations of my spiritual journey.

To David Laws, Christine Rose and June Davies who also walk the same spiritual path of helping others – you will always hold a special place in my heart.

Thanks to Wendy Stuart of Wendy & Words, my editor, and her husband Peter. I cannot thank you enough for your assistance in bringing this book to life.

About the Author

Julie Capri is an Australian Psychic Medium Channeler, artist, ET Contactee, and speaker in the fields of spiritual growth, self-development, and Extras Terrestrial and Extra Dimensional Beings.

Her new book *Awakening – It's your time to remember who you really are* includes the essence of her Awakening Teachings, which have been brought forth to awaken the consciousness of mankind and bring us a new level of awareness upon Earth.

With 30 years of passion and dedication to spiritual advancement, Julie has been elevating her consciousness to higher realms beyond the boundaries of physical existence. She now shares her knowledge with the world.

Contact Julie Capri:
Email: info@juliecapri.com
Website: www.juliecapri.com